The Alchemy of Letting Go

The Alchemy of Letting Go

AMBER MORRELL

Albert Whitman & Company
Chicago, Illinois

Library of Congress Cataloging-in-Publication data is on file with the publisher.

Text copyright © 2023 by Amber Morrell
First published in the United States of America in 2023 by Albert Whitman & Company
ISBN 978-0-8075-4937-7 (hardcover)
ISBN 978-0-8075-4938-4 (ebook)
Printed in the United States of America
10 9 8 7 6 5 4 3 2 1 LB 28 27 26 25 24 23

Jacket art copyright © 2023 by Albert Whitman & Company
Jacket art by James Firnhaber
Design by Erin McMahon

For more information about Albert Whitman & Company,
visit our website at www.albertwhitman.com.

For my daughter, Penelope,
who is made of magic—AM

PART I
Observe

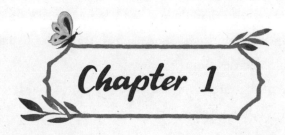

Chapter 1

My living room is full of dead bugs.

My parents are entomologists. The living room is where they do the majority of their work. I'm an entomologist too—I can recite more arthropod families than some of my father's college students. Call them what you want: bugs, insects, creepy-crawlies. Those are what entomologists study. And those are what fills the dozens of glass cases in my family's living room.

I sneak down from my bedroom before Mom or Dad wake up. Gray light leaks from the window. I stop in front of each display case to bid the bugs good morning.

The cases are organized by type. We've got beetles, spiders, and my favorite, lepidoptera: butterflies and moths. There are thousands of different kinds, and my parents have hundreds of samples, pinned and labeled in my father's meticulous hand. But there's one butterfly that always catches my eye. It's smaller than a quarter and has blue gossamer wings—thin, filmy, delicate.

The Palos Verdes Blue.

It's one of the rarest butterflies in the world and lives only in the coastal watershed near my house—if you can find it. Dad's sample was bred in captivity, and he had to fill out mountains of paperwork to get it. But that's not the same as finding one in the wild. It's not a real Palos Verdes Blue.

I run my fingers over the glass, like I do every morning. I look at my own collection in the next case over. There is a blank space and a handwritten label. My sister, Ingrid, wrote it three years ago when we first started secretly hunting for the Blue. *G. lygdamus palosverdesensis.* I'm going to fill that spot with a real wild Palos Verdes Blue, if it's the last thing I do.

It's time to get to work. I pull out my notebooks and well-worn maps of the nature preserve. Our seventh-grade life science class is going on a field trip to learn about biomes for our class project, but I'm not going to waste this opportunity. I would hate to catch a glimpse of a Blue and not be ready to catch it. If Ingrid were still here, she wouldn't go into the situation unprepared.

I pack the rest of my supplies: my butterfly net, a jar, some plastic baggies, and a lunch box packed carefully with ice. If I find one, I want to preserve it as best I can.

I hear footsteps on the stairs and shove my gear under the desk before the overhead light flickers on. Dad stands in the doorway.

"You're up early again."

His voice cracks with early morning grogginess, like it always does before he has his coffee. He wears a big T-shirt with the university entomology department logo on it, and the dragonfly-print pajama pants I got him for Father's Day last year.

"It's never too early for science." I stand with my legs blocking the desk.

"Well, *this* scientist debates that theory." He turns around and heads into the kitchen. A moment later, I hear the coffee grinder growl to life.

Of course Dad supports my scientific ventures, but I know he wouldn't be happy with me taking my gear to school. I'm not supposed to catch a Palos Verdes Blue; they're an endangered species, after all. Dad says catching a wild Blue does nothing to advance science. But it was important to Ingrid, and Ingrid was a brilliant scientist.

The only thing I didn't pack is my notebook. It's filled with maps and the field notes Ingrid and I made over the years. I clutch it tightly, my most prized possession.

I gulp down a bowl of cereal while Dad gets ready for work. Mom comes down and gets herself a cup of coffee.

"Slow down, June," she says. "At least look at your food while you eat it."

I shrug, one hand shoveling in frosted flakes while the other holds down the pages of my notebook.

Dad comes back downstairs, dressed in dark denim jeans and a brown jacket with elbow patches. My parents chitchat about their plans for the day—Mom talks about a lecture she's giving later at the science museum, and Dad complains about some of his students at the university not turning in their papers. I bounce from foot to foot as I wait by the door, imagining my net coming down on shimmering blue wings. I can't get the image out of my mind.

I say goodbye to Mom and follow Dad out to his car. The neighborhood stray cat watches me from the lawn. He's all gray, except for his tail, which is striped black and a little too long for his body. His big yellow eyes follow me to the car. As we pull out of the driveway, he disappears into the bushes on the side of our yard.

When we pull up to the school, Dad clears his throat.

"You know, it's not too late to change your mind about today."

"No way." I clutch my backpack closer to my chest. "I'll be fine."

I jump out of the car before Dad can say anything else. He doesn't like the nature preserve—not after what happened to Ingrid. He doesn't know that I ride my bike there most afternoons, trying to get a glimpse of the Blue. I wave goodbye and join the line of seventh-grade students waiting to board a big yellow bus.

I keep my head buried in my field notebook, so I don't notice Mateo Michaelson when he slides next to me onto the stiff bench seat. Mateo started at our school a few months ago, but he doesn't really have any friends yet. He always has his head buried in a book, his messy brown curls peeking up above the pages. I catch a glimpse of the book he's reading now; it's a journal, with lines of swoopy handwriting covering the pages.

Before I can get a good look, Mrs. Cartwright, our science teacher, makes announcements about field trip safety from the front of the bus. I open my own notebook and flip through my maps of the nature preserve. As the bus starts down the road, I try to block out the sounds of the other kids shouting and laughing. When we go around a corner, Mateo's shoulder bumps into mine.

"Sorry." He scoots over a bit, but there's not much space. His eyes wander to my notebook. "What's that?"

"Notes." Irritated, I turn the page. The next page has a sketch of the Palos Verdes Blue that I did in colored pencil.

"Hey, that's really good," he says. "Do you like to draw?"

"Only when I need to. For record keeping." The next few pages are entries of observations from my previous excursions. Most of the time, the Blue escapes me, so I write down where I go and what I see. But occasionally I catch a flash of blue wings, and in those moments my handwriting grows to match my excitement. Every entry is a step closer to catching one.

"Is that, like, a butterfly diary, then?"

I shut the notebook and look up at Mateo. His eyes are deep brown with flecks of gold in them, like the wings of a Brown

Hairstreak. His own notebook is still open in his lap, his fountain pen tapping anxiously against his knee.

"It's not a diary," I snap. "It's for observing the natural world."

He blinks as if he doesn't understand, then shrugs.

"Same thing, right?"

"No. It's really not."

I open my notebook back up to my maps. I've highlighted the routes where the Blue has been spotted. Today we'll be walking along one of the creek-side trails and learning about watersheds. I scan the map to find the exact route, and my heart sinks when I realize where the path will take us.

No. It can't be. The nature preserve covers several square miles. Why do we have to take this particular trail? I trace the path along the stream to the ocean and take a deep breath.

It will be okay. Once I'm out there among the milkweeds, I won't even be thinking about Ingrid.

The air buzzes with excitement as the bus pulls up to the nature preserve's main parking lot. I want to get off this bus and get away from Mateo's prying brown eyes. When we file off the bus, Mrs. Cartwright calls off names two by two, pairing us up with a buddy for the science project.

I hate group projects. I know I can make an excellent presentation all on my own. I won first prize in the school science fair last year, even against the seventh and eighth graders. Working with other people is a waste of time.

Mateo skips off to meet his partner. I adjust my sun hat as

Mrs. Cartwright calls my name.

"Juniper Edwards and Chelsea Coville."

Her voice continues to rattle off names, but I stand frozen. Not Chelsea. Anyone but Chelsea. This day is getting worse and worse.

A girl with blond hair in two long braids tied with flowers walks up to me. She's wearing a T-shirt for a cartoon I don't recognize. She's drawn all over her arms and her shoes in marker. Everything about Chelsea is busy, jumbled, and disorganized. She makes my head spin.

"Hi, Juniper!" Her voice is loud, high-pitched, bubbly. I can't meet her blue eyes. "Looks like the band's back together, huh?"

Chelsea was my best friend all through elementary school. But she started taking art lessons and going to concerts and acting in school plays, and I became a scientist. We drifted apart.

"Guess so," I say, forcing a smile.

I look around and breathe in the ocean air. I can't see the water from here, but I can hear the seagulls above us, and some Common Buckeyes flutter nearby. Everything is green and fresh and beautiful. We got a lot more rain than usual this winter, which led to a lush spring. I pull out my binoculars and loop them around my neck to see the Buckeyes better without getting in trouble for wandering away.

"Wow, you look like an explorer," Chelsea says. The two friends standing beside her nod in agreement. They're wearing brightly colored clothes and a million accessories—layers of hair clips and bracelets and necklaces. I look down at my khakis.

"I wanted to be comfortable on the hike."

Chelsea's eyes go wide. "We're hiking?"

Mrs. Cartwright appears beside us. She's wearing khaki cargo shorts and has a wide-brimmed hat of her own, and I don't feel so out of place. "Yes, Chelsea, the purpose of visiting a nature trail is to walk on it. Now, start walking. We have to meet the tour guide in front of the nature center."

Chelsea and her friends skip up the path, already forgetting about my existence. That's fine with me. I hang back and study my map.

"Juniper."

I look up. Mrs. Cartwright looks at me the way adults tend to look at me these days—with concern. But she shouldn't. I'm a great student. I have a 102 in science.

"I know you take science seriously, and I'm proud of you for that. But try to have fun today, okay? Get your nose out of your maps and stop and smell the flowers."

To demonstrate, she leans over to smell some bright yellow bush sunflowers, then gestures for me to do the same. I take an exaggerated sniff.

"I'll try."

"And don't wander." Mrs. Cartwright smiles and walks ahead to meet the tour guide.

Mrs. Cartwright wants me to have fun and relax, but I can't. I have work to do. She doesn't understand how important finding a Palos Verdes Blue is to me. She's never seen the blank space in my collection, the label written in Ingrid's neatest handwriting. If I'm going to smell flowers, I'll smell them after I catch our butterfly.

I don't listen to the tour guide drone on about trail safety. I know the nature preserve as well as I know my own house. When the hike begins, Chelsea and her friends hang back so they can talk without the teacher noticing, and I walk close behind them. Milkweeds, buckwheat, and poppies sprout in the brush around us. The warm air buzzes with bees and other insects. Chelsea and her friends scream when a bee gets too close, but bees don't bother me. When one buzzes near my ear, I don't even flinch.

A Buckeye lands on a milkweed leaf beside the path, and I stop to get a closer look. It folds and unfolds its wings slowly before it flutters back into the air and zips away again.

"Juniper, keep up!" Chelsea glares back at me, her arms linked with her two friends. They've stopped in a wide dirt clearing and gathered around the tour guide, who is saying something I can't quite hear.

Here the path splits into two. One goes up a small hill, higher onto the peninsula and ultimately to the cliffs, while the other stays low, following the creek all the way down to the ocean. I hear the rumble of water over rock. All that extra rain means the creek is much deeper and louder than usual.

The rushing water drowns out the sound of the tour guide, and if I look away, I can imagine I'm alone here.

11

Blue flashes in the corner of my eye.

It's gone as fast as it arrived, but I know what I saw. I shove my notebook into my pocket and put my binoculars to my eyes. Palos Verdes Blues are as small as a quarter and fast, which is why they're so hard to catch. I look up the sloping path and then around to the lower path. Nothing. I put my binoculars down and huff.

Blue wings flutter right in front of me. There it is. The Palos Verdes Blue.

It's on the back of Chelsea's head.

I take a careful step forward. I don't have time to pull out my net. I cup my hands and lift them slowly. I'll have to be gentle—

"Juniper! Pay attention, please!"

Mrs. Cartwright's voice makes Chelsea spin around, and the Blue flutters away. I swing, whacking Chelsea in the face. The Blue is in the air now, higher, higher, out of reach—gone.

"Ow! What the heck!" Chelsea rubs her forehead, but her voice is low.

"Sorry," I mumble.

Mrs. Cartwright eyes us suspiciously.

I scan the sky, but the Palos Verdes Blue is out of sight. I clench my fists.

I had a perfect chance, and I blew it.

The group starts to move toward the left, taking the higher path away from the creek. But there's a lot more milkweeds, the plants butterflies like most, by the water. My heart beats fast

12

from my close encounter with the Blue. Now I know there's one nearby, and I know I can find it again.

I shuffle my feet as I follow the group, falling a little behind. I hold my hand over my eyes to block the sun as I scan the plants around me. And then I spot it: gossamer wings perched on a leaf, relaxing among the milkweeds down beside the creek. Waiting for me to catch it.

I glance up. Everyone's busy complaining about hiking up the hill; no one is paying attention to me. I can slip away, catch the Blue, and slide back into the group without anyone noticing.

Mrs. Cartwright said not to wander, but I don't know when I'll get another chance to find a Blue. I turn and walk quickly to the lower path, my boots kicking up dirt.

"Where are you going?" Chelsea's voice makes me jump. She's following me.

"I'll catch up," I say, brushing her off. "You go."

But she doesn't. She follows me until we're out of sight of the rest of the group, and the only sounds around us are the creek and the birdsong.

"I'm your buddy," she says. "If I lose you, I'll get in trouble."

"I'm not lost."

Between the path and the water is a dense thicket of milk-weeds. I see the Blue, folding and unfolding its delicate wings on a branch overhanging the creek. I step off the path, leaves crunching beneath my feet as I pick my way through the bushes.

"Hey!" Chelsea shouts. "They said not to go off the path."

I ignore her, my eyes focused on the Blue. This is it. The one butterfly I've searched for, the one that will complete our collection. The one that will make Ingrid proud of me. I step forward, hands gripped around the butterfly net, ready to swing.

My foot catches on a rock, and I tumble forward into the water.

Chapter 2

Here are the scientific facts of what happens when you drown, which I learned during swimming lessons last summer:

1. YOUR VOCAL CORDS SPASM AND BLOCK YOUR AIRWAYS TO PROTECT YOUR LUNGS.
2. NOT ENOUGH OXYGEN REACHES YOUR ORGANS.
3. YOU BECOME UNCONSCIOUS.
4. YOUR LUNGS FILL WITH WATER, AND YOU SUFFOCATE.

All these facts fill my mind as I struggle to get to the surface. I flail my arms and legs, but my backpack weighs me down. I try to shuck it off, but I can't get my arms out. The binoculars' cord pulls painfully on my neck. My chest hurts. My eyes hurt. I don't know which way is up.

This is it.

This is just how Ingrid died.

And now I'm going to die too.

I feel sleepy. I can't move my arms or my legs anymore. I float, and it feels like I'm floating forever. I see something at the bottom of the creek bed. It's bright green, and it's glowing with eerie light.

What could it be? There are no bioluminescent creatures here. We learned about bioluminescent algae a few months ago. They create their own light and look like glowsticks underwater. But those are in the ocean, not here. My mind drifts sleepily. I close my eyes, but the green light still pulses in my vision.

The water becomes shockingly cold and icy. I wonder if that's a side effect of drowning. My teeth chatter down onto my tongue.

Arms wrap around me, and warm air shocks me into focus. Someone drags me onto the dry bank. My throat burns as I cough up water and bile. Everything hurts—my throat is raw, my eyes sting, and there's an annoying pounding in my ears. And voices. So many voices.

My body feels heavy, and I roll over onto my back. The sun is directly in my eyes, so I close them. I feel the dirt sticking to me, all over my body, the way that metal sand at the science museum sticks to a giant magnet.

"Juniper? Juniper, can you hear me?"

It's Mrs. Cartwright's voice. I open my eyes and see her blurry face blocking the sun. I try to croak out an answer, but all I can manage is a raspy cough. Her fingers touch my neck.

"She's breathing."

Mrs. Cartwright stands up and starts talking in a quick, low voice to someone. I close my eyes. Somewhere far away, I hear sirens.

Behind my eyelids, I can see the green light. It ebbs, flows, and crashes like waves, and no matter how tightly I squeeze my eyes, it doesn't go away. There are so many voices. I don't open my eyes until I feel strong, unfamiliar arms lifting me up. I think about telling them I'm okay, that I can walk on my own, but I don't. I don't want the green light to go away. It's comforting. I keep my eyes closed, letting the light wash over me while the paramedic carries me to the ambulance.

In the back of the ambulance, machines whir and beep while the paramedics look me over. They replace my wet shirt with a giant T-shirt from the nature preserve's gift shop. Funnily enough, it says SAVE THE PALOS VERDES BLUE in giant letters and has a big blue butterfly on the front. Right now, it isn't the Blue that needs saving.

The cold metal of the stethoscope makes me shiver as it slides across my back. The paramedic makes a bunch of notes on a clipboard. Mrs. Cartwright stands outside the ambulance doors, looking anxious. She doesn't say anything, but I know that I'm in big trouble.

"Everything's looking good." The paramedic is a short man with a deep voice. "I don't think we'll need to transport her to the hospital today, but there are a few things she'll need to keep an eye on over the next twenty-four hours."

A blue car pulls up beside the ambulance. I've never been so grateful and so scared to see my dad's car. He hops out, face crumpled.

"That's her father," Mrs. Cartwright tells the paramedic.

"Perfect. I'll explain everything to him."

The paramedic and Mrs. Cartwright leave me seated on the gurney while they go talk to my dad. I can't hear what they're saying—there's still water in my ears—but I can feel my dad's eyes on me. I can't meet his gaze.

My sopping wet backpack sits in the corner. Someone must have fished it out of the creek. Lying on top is my notebook. I hop down from the gurney to pick it up. The pages are all wrinkled, and when I open it up all the words are smeared and unreadable.

I've been working on this notebook for years. It's the most important thing I own. The first several pages were written by Ingrid, and now they're ruined and irreplaceable. Gone forever.

When Ingrid died, I promised that I would pick up where she left off. I promised I would find the Blue and finally finish what she started. I didn't have her, but I had her notes, her work. And now I have nothing.

Ingrid drowned here two years ago. An accident, the police

said. But we never really knew what happened. How must Dad feel, to get a phone call that his other child almost drowned in the same place?

The ambulance groans as my dad steps up into the back.

"Hey, June."

He's not mad, and somehow that makes it worse.

"I'm sorry," I whisper.

He pulls me into a hug and rubs my back, his warm arms comforting and familiar.

"It's okay," he says. "You're all right. It's going to be okay."

I can't tell if the words are for me or for him. I want to feel guilty—I know that I should. But all I can think about is the Blue fluttering just out of reach. If I'd only reached a little farther...

After a moment he pulls away.

"Let's get you home, okay? I'll make you some tea. We'll watch a movie. *Bee Movie*, huh? Your favorite?"

Bee Movie is not my favorite movie, and Dad knows this. He only says it to get me to smile, so I do.

"But what about your class?"

He waves his hand dismissively.

"I sent them all home. They'll survive till Thursday."

Dad helps me up and picks up my wet backpack. My butterfly net is nowhere to be found. It's probably rushing down the creek on its way to polluting the ocean—another thing I should feel guilty for, but maybe it's for the best. If I had been caught with my net, I'd be in even deeper trouble.

I sit baking in the hot car for a few minutes while Dad talks to Mrs. Cartwright. I can't hear what they're saying but I'm not sure I want to anyway.

I lean back and close my eyes and scratch at my itchy legs. I'm still wearing my soaked cargo pants. It's impossible to scratch through wet fabric. As I try, my fingers bump something hard in my pocket.

Strange. I don't remember having anything in my pockets other than my notebook, which is now shoved into my backpack, ruined. I reach inside my pocket and feel something small and cold.

I pull it out, and the car is filled with an emerald-green light. I'd forgotten about that light—I thought it was a hallucination. When your brain doesn't get enough oxygen, sometimes you see things that aren't really there.

But in my hand is the stone, solid and real.

My whole body goes cold, as if I've plunged into the creek once again.

I don't have time to examine it before Dad opens the car door. I hide my hand behind my back, the stone clutched tightly in my fist. My heart thrums in my ears. This isn't some rock I found on the ground and put into my pocket for safekeeping. It *appeared* there. It doesn't make sense, and I don't like things without an explanation.

Dad turns the key in the ignition and begins the long drive home. We're not that far—on a good day, I can ride my bike to the nature preserve from my house in less than twenty minutes. In a car it takes only seven minutes, unless you hit every red light. Which we do.

Dad isn't talking. I'm not talking. The paramedic says I will be fine as long as I don't have trouble breathing for the next twenty-four hours. I can breathe okay, but I don't feel fine. My head hurts. I feel dizzy.

And then there's the stone.

Normally when I find something interesting, Dad is the first person I show it to. He likes examining strange things, like the shapes of seashells or the patterns on moths' wings. He always stops and notices the little things in the world. But this is different. I can't be excited about this when he's so upset.

At a red light Dad finally breaks the silence.

"How are you feeling?"

I use my free hand to tuck some damp hair behind my ear.

"Fine."

I force a small smile, and he smiles back. The only sound in the car is the clicking of the turn signal. I can't say anything else. I don't want to make my dad worry any more than I already have.

I look out the window instead of looking at him. Watching the mailboxes and crisp green lawns zip by helps me feel a little less dizzy. They give my eyes something to focus on, to forget how inexplicable the glowing stone is. When we turn onto my street, I notice something else that doesn't make sense.

The abandoned house next door looks different. I barely

glanced at it this morning, but it was the same as it always was: boarded-up windows and rusted fence, chipping paint and overgrown yard. But now it looks like it's gotten a fresh coat of paint. All the boards are off the windows, too, and the yard is trimmed.

"Is someone moving in?" I ask.

The car jerks as Dad puts on the parking brake.

"What?"

"To the old Elm House." I gesture at it through the window. We call it the Elm House because of the two large elm trees in the front yard. "It looks like it's being remodeled."

Dad leans over me and squints out the window.

"Looks the same to me." His eyebrows wrinkle together as he looks at me. "Let's go inside and get you some rest, yeah?"

I look back at the Elm House. It looks different than this morning, I'm sure of it. From here, over the fence and hedges, I can only see the third floor. Under the gabled roof, there's a window. In that window, there's a light.

I catch a shape darting into the bushes—that old stray cat again. But it looks different too. Its yellow eyes look bigger, and its tail seems longer. I shiver, even though the sun is warm on my skin. I follow Dad slowly up the driveway to the house. I don't dare open my fingers to look at the stone.

Chapter 3

I shut my bedroom door and tip my head back against it. I take a deep breath and count to ten before I let it out. It's something Ingrid taught me, to calm down. When I exhale, I walk to my desk. It's covered in papers, jars, and bug samples. I find a clear spot and set the stone down.

The entire room fills with green light as soon as I move my hand away. I lean in to get a closer look. It looks like a normal rock, smoothed out by the flow of the water. I'm not a geologist, but I can't think of any scientific reason for it to be glowing.

But that is impossible. There is *always* a scientific explanation. I just have to figure it out.

There are seven basic steps to the scientific method:

1. OBSERVE
2. QUESTION
3. HYPOTHESIZE
4. EXPERIMENT
5. ANALYZE
6. REPEAT
7. CONCLUDE

I know that if I follow these seven steps, I'll have my answer. Science hasn't failed me yet.

I open the bottom drawer of my desk, where I keep a stack of notebooks. Some are for documenting insects, and some are about experiments I want to try, but I know that this is unlike anything I've experienced before. I pull out a fresh, blank notebook and flip to the first page.

Pencil in hand, I stare at the stone. What do I know so far? The surface looks gray but emits a green light. I saw it on the bottom of the creek, and then it somehow made its way into my pocket. Some things look different: the Elm House, the stray cat. Are those related? I write them all down.

I ponder over all this while I change my clothes. The most likely answer is that I suffered some sort of head injury that hasn't been detected yet. I don't feel any pain, but maybe that's part of the delusion. The green light shimmers from the stone, like smoke from a candle, wispy and wavering. The color is so vibrant. If this is a delusion, I must have hit my head really, *really* hard.

Something taps against my window. My eyes flick to the closed blinds. Maybe it was the wind…but then I hear it again. Tap, tap, tap.

I take a deep breath. I want to count to ten again, but the tapping won't stop. Tap, tap, tap. A bird, maybe—do woodpeckers live around here? I don't know enough about avian fauna. Tap, tap, tap. I yank open the blinds.

Perched on the red roof tiles is the stray cat.

Except it's not.

My brain knows that this is the same stray cat as before. It has the same long, striped tail, the same gray fur, and the same yellow eyes. But the creature outside my window is not a cat at all. It's a lemur. Specifically, *Lemur catta*, a ring-tailed lemur.

It looks at me with unblinking yellow eyes that are rimmed with black fur. It has a white face and a black snout and a small gray-and-white body. Its tail, twice as long as its body and striped with black and gray, flicks back and forth as it stares through the window.

Lemur catta are native to Madagascar, an island off the eastern coast of Africa. I learned that when Mom gave tours for the African animal exhibit at the natural history museum. I'm not an African animal expert, either, but I know that there are no lemurs in Southern California except at the zoo. I can't do anything but stare back.

The lemur cocks its head at me, then looks down at the glowing stone on my desk. Its expression doesn't change. Do lemurs have facial expressions? It presses its small hands against the window. They look strangely like human hands, but somehow, I'm not afraid. After all, I'm probably hallucinating this entire scenario. So I open the window.

The lemur hops inside, landing lightly on my desk, surprisingly graceful. Then it sits back on its hind legs and looks up at me. A deep voice comes out of its mouth.

"Hello, Juniper. It's nice to finally meet you."

I blink at it. I'm definitely hallucinating. Lemurs don't talk—and if they did, they wouldn't have British accents.

"Ah, my apologies," the lemur continues. "It must be a bit of a shock to see someone such as myself in your bedroom. The name's Soren."

The lemur holds out his hand, but I don't move.

"You can talk."

Soren rolls his eyes.

"Yes, yes, I can talk. Have your moment of shock, but please do it quickly, because I have pertinent information to impart."

A small, fuzzy foot taps impatiently against my desk. My heart pounds in my chest. Observe, I tell myself. Observe and breathe. I look around my room to see if anything else is out of place. There's the glowing stone, of course, but other than that, everything looks perfectly normal. The untidy stacks of papers, the laundry on my desk chair, the vintage insect sketches pinned to the walls. Nothing else looks like it's about to start talking. There must be some sort of explanation.

"What's happening?" My voice is a lot more scared than I meant for it to sound.

Soren gestures to the stone.

"What you have there, I'm sure you realize, is no ordinary rock."

He leans down, the green glow illuminating his furry face, and stretches a clawed finger toward it. I feel suddenly panicked—I can't let him touch the stone.

"Don't—!"

He pulls his hand back and smirks. A lemur smirking is a very unnatural and uncomfortable thing to witness, too human-like for an animal. Soren jumps down from his perch on my desk and scampers to the top of my chair, where we can look eye to eye.

"You feel it, then? A connection between yourself and the stone."

Is that what this feeling is? A connection? I look down at the stone and feel drawn to it, like the pull of two magnets not quite close enough to touch. I shake my head—it must be an illusion.

"No, I just—I don't know what it is. But I will figure it out. There must be a scientific explanation."

Soren leans in secretively.

"I know where you can get answers, you know. And it's not too far."

"Where?"

Soren jerks his head toward the window.

"The house next door."

A chill wind blows through the window. I thought the house looked different, but there's no way so many renovations could have been done on it since this morning. And besides, Dad said no one moved in.

"No one lives next door."

"Someone has always lived next door. They've just been very good at hiding it from those without magic. And you're not without magic anymore, are you?"

"You're not making any sense," I scoff. "What do you mean, magic?"

Soren picks up a pen from my desk and twirls it around his fingers.

"You know. Magic. The kind of thing that lets you find glowing stones and talk to wild animals."

"No," I say, backing away. "That's impossible."

Soren brandishes the pen at me like a sword.

"Is this conversation we are having impossible?"

"Yes. It's all in my head. I must've hit it when I fell. There's a perfectly logical reason for all of this." I gesture at the room around me. "For you. The stone. Everything. There has to be."

Soren jumps back onto the desk and taps the pen against the window.

"Your answers are there, when you're ready."

Footsteps sound on the stairs. I forgot about Dad. I grab the stone off my desk and shove it into my pocket. I spin around just as the door opens to see my dad holding a steaming mug of tea.

"Everything all right, Juniper? I made—hey! What's that cat doing in here?"

Dad waves his free hand around, sloshing tea onto the floor in the process. Soren scampers out the window.

"Shoo!" Dad goes to the window and slams it shut, narrowly missing Soren's tail.

"What were you thinking, letting that cat in? Mom's allergic, you know."

Outside the window, Soren the lemur winks a wide yellow eye before disappearing over the edge of the roof.

"Sorry," I mumble. "It was an accident."

Dad lets out a long breath, then looks down at the tea. The mug is only half full now.

"Well, I'll get some towels and put your clothes in the wash. You relax, okay?"

Downstairs, Dad has set out a nest of blankets on the couch, so I settle in and turn on the television. I scroll mindlessly through the movie options, unable to focus.

The fact that he saw Soren as a normal cat proves it: I'm hallucinating. I'll have to tell Dad that I need to go to the hospital and get my head checked. But as I scroll with the remote in my right hand, my left hand goes mindlessly to my pocket. I turn the stone over and over in my palm. It feels very cold and very real.

Chapter 4

When I walk into school the next day, I feel the other kids looking at me. They whisper my name, and I try my best to ignore it. It's easy during first-period math. Focusing on the numbers gives me the distraction I need. When I turn in my quiz at the end of class, I think maybe today won't be so bad.

But next period is English, which happens to be my worst subject.

I slide into the desk I always use, in the farthest row next to the windows, about halfway back. I like sitting by the window because English is incredibly dull. I'm terrible at identifying things like "subtext" and "theme." Why should I care about books written two hundred years ago when I'm much more fascinated by things happening right now? Give me an encyclopedia on native Californian plants and I'll happily read that before anything by Charles Dickens. In fact, I have. It's called *The Jepson Manual*, and I've read it three times.

Currently we are doing a unit on poetry, which is the worst. Words don't mean what they're supposed to mean, and all the poems are about feelings I don't want to feel.

I'm staring out the window when Mateo slips into the desk in front of me. A crow pecks at an abandoned fast-food bag by the chain-link fence. Mateo twists around to face me, but I don't look at him.

"Hey, Juniper."

I flit my eyes to him before glancing back to the crow, which is more interesting than Mateo's big, worried eyes. I don't want his concern; I want him to mind his own business.

"Hi," I say flatly.

"You doing okay? After…" He clears his throat.

"I'm fine." I don't want to talk about anything that happened yesterday, especially as more kids start to fill the room. "Really, I am."

Mateo nods, but he doesn't look convinced. I'm not fine. The stone pulses in my pocket. There was no reason for me to bring it to school, but I didn't want anything to happen to it while I was gone. What if Mom or Dad found it? It needs further study, and until I get answers, I'm not letting it out of my sight.

"So what *really* happened?" Mateo whispers. "What were you doing when you fell?"

I look back out the window. The crow pulls its head out of the bag and flies away, a French fry clutched in its beak.

"I don't want to talk about it."

It's not that I'm ashamed of being an entomologist. Most people don't know enough about butterflies to know that I'm technically not supposed to catch a Palos Verdes Blue, since it's an endangered species. But I know that butterfly hunting is not what Mateo wants to know about. When he asks me what happened, it's the exact same question people asked me when Ingrid died: What *really* happened? Why was she there all alone?

No one knows that answer except for Ingrid, and she's gone.

"So, um, are you ready for the quiz today?" Mateo asks, changing the subject.

I snap my gaze back to him just as the bell rings.

"What quiz?"

Mateo's eyes widen.

"On Langston Hughes—"

"All right, y'all," Mr. Harris says, clapping his hands together. "I hope you finished reading your packet."

Mr. Harris wears a button-down shirt and a tie, like he always does on test days. He says that if students have to come to class prepared for a quiz, then so should he.

I am not prepared. I haven't even glanced at the Langston Hughes packet. As Mr. Harris passes out quizzes, my heart accelerates in a panic. He slips a quiz in front of me, pausing for a moment to raise his eyebrows. I'm not sure if it's because of the look of terror on my face or the fact that I've gotten, at best, a C on every quiz in his class.

I write my name in neat, precise script at the top of my paper, taking my time. I tap my pencil nervously as I skim over the first few questions. They're all about a poem called "Harlem." A poem I never read a single line of.

I'm going to fail.

Mr. Harris leans back in his chair and props his feet up on his desk next to pot of white flowers and a framed picture of his cat. He pulls out a thick mystery novel. I scan the room— everyone scribbles quickly on their papers, heads bent low. If the quiz were multiple choice, I would have a statistically good chance of getting some right just by luck. But all these questions are short answer.

I'm doomed.

I take a few deep breaths. It's okay. I'll study extra hard for the next one. Maybe I can still save my grade. I can't stop a sinking feeling in the pit of my stomach. After losing the Blue, falling into the creek, finding glowing rocks, and talking to lemurs, failing this test is the cherry on top of an already terrible week.

I roll the pencil around in my fingers, trying to figure out how I'm going to come up with any answers. Something twitches against my hand. I look at my pencil. There's something weird about it. It was just a normal yellow pencil, with a pink eraser at the bottom and a freshly sharpened tip. But its smooth yellow coating is no longer smooth—it's covered in bumps and cracks as if it were chewed up.

Then I realize it's *moving*.

I drop the pencil on my desk as the yellow surface bubbles and cracks, revealing something pale white. At first I think it's a larva—the baby stage of lepidoptera. But why would there be larvae inside my pencil? I brush the wiggly white thing away, and it disappears off the side of the desk. Then it happens again. Small *somethings* start erupting from all over the pencil, to the point where it no longer looks like a pencil at all. And I realize that they're not larvae—they're the sprouts of a plant.

Everyone's too busy with their quiz to notice...or maybe they don't see what I see at all, like how Dad saw Soren as a normal cat. I don't want to find out. I hide the pencil in my lap and watch as a dozen little stems pop up and squirm around, searching for sunlight. I try to brush the sprouts away, but every time I uproot one, another replaces it. I shove the pencil into my backpack.

The surface of my desk cracks.

I let out an involuntary squeak, and several heads turn in my direction, Mateo's included. His eyes widen. Mr. Harris peeks over the top of his book, and I cover the cracks with my quiz.

"Do you need something, Juniper?"

I shake my head, trying to look as innocent as possible, as if everything I touch isn't mysteriously growing.

Then I see the flowers next to Mr. Harris's feet. The leaves tremble and the soil churns. Mr. Harris doesn't seem to notice, even as roots spill over the sides of the pot.

I don't know how or why this is happening, but I do know one thing: I need to get out of here.

"Can I use the bathroom? Please?"

Mr. Harris glares at me over the top of his square glasses.

"Are you finished with your quiz?"

I look down at my still-blank quiz. Green tufts of moss have started spreading over the white paper. I try to wipe them off, and they smear like green ink.

"It's an emergency!"

Before Mr. Harris can argue, I grab my backpack and sprint to the door. I don't look back.

I dash down the hallway to the girls' bathroom. It's the only place I can think of where I can be away from everyone. I dig the pencil out of my backpack. It's wrapped with spiraling vines, leaves, and little white flowers. I throw it into the trash and shove it down as deep as I can.

But that doesn't stop it. Vines pour over the sides of the trash can. Suddenly, the paper towels fly out of the dispenser, shifting and changing into leaves. They flutter around the air like a million green wings. Not even the bathroom is safe. I run back out into the hall, my backpack only half slung over my shoulder.

As I run past the office, the secretary calls after me. I ignore her. I push open the double doors and run down the concrete steps, sprinting across the lawn toward the street. Shouted voices make me look back. Little white flowers erupt in my footprints.

I feel like I'm going to throw up, even though I skipped

breakfast this morning. This is all wrong. Plants don't grow this way. My feet thud against the pavement as I run, rattling my teeth. I don't think about where I'm going. I just want to get away. I decide that home is the safest choice.

I cut across the park to get to my street faster, and I almost trip. Vines grow in thick tangles around my feet. Behind me, my entire path is lined with flowers, leaves, and overgrown grass. A trail of brilliant, earthy green.

Green. I reach into my pocket and pull out the stone. It's still as cold as the frigid creek water, and even in the sunlight it glows as bright as ever.

Could this stone be the reason all of this is happening? Is it the reason I ditched school and probably failed English for good?

I've never given up on a research challenge, but for once, I don't want answers. I want everything to go back to normal.

I weigh the stone in my palm, then chuck it across the park as hard as I can. It disappears in the grass. I keep running.

But the unexplained growing doesn't stop. Plants swell in the corner of my eye. I brush my pocket with my fingers, and I realize that the stone is there again.

This can't be real. It's impossible. Everything in this world has a reason, an explanation. It's our job as scientists—as *humans*—to study and learn those reasons, to gain a greater understanding of our universe. At least, that's what I believed when I woke up yesterday morning.

Now, as I round the corner of my block to the now-beautiful

Elm House, everything I thought was true is uncertain. I pause in front of the gate of the old house. There is a light in the highest window. A shadow passes in front of the light, just for a moment. It's human-sized, not lemur-sized. Who else lives in that house other than Soren? I take the stone out of my pocket again and chuck it over the fence.

If the weird house and its mysterious inhabitants want it, they can have it.

I run up the driveway of my own house, careful to avoid the lawn. Once I'm inside I lock the door. Mom's at the museum; Dad's at the university. Usually I don't mind being alone in the house, but today I miss Ingrid. Ingrid was always there for me. The loving, protective big sister. If she'd seen me run out of school in a panic, she would've been right behind me.

But Ingrid is gone.

I walk into the living room. The walls are covered in display cases. Hundreds of butterflies, beetles, and other arthropods stare back at me—Ingrid's friends, and mine too.

I walk over to Dad's display case, where he has a specimen of a Palos Verdes Blue. I touch my fingertips to the glass. I remember when Ingrid first told Dad she wanted to catch one of her own. I remember the defiant fire in her eyes when he told her he already had one, and she said, "No. It was raised in a butterfly house, not the wild. It's not the same. It's not *real.*"

Dad was definitely against it, but that didn't make her stop trying to catch one—she just kept it a secret. Something special between me and her. Once Ingrid was gone, I swore that I would catch a real Palos Verdes Blue. For her. For us.

I wish Ingrid were here. She would know what to do.

Behind the glass, a shimmering blue wing twitches. I rub my eyes. A trick of the light. But then it moves again, and I realize every specimen in the case of twenty-six butterflies squirms, pulling up at their pins.

I thought I was safe inside the house, but whatever this is—this magic, Soren called it—isn't limited to plants.

I stumble backward and bump into the end table. I put my hand out to steady myself, and it knocks the case of butterflies off the wall. It falls to the ground with a smash.

Broken glass and butterfly specimens sprawl across the floor. The glass stays put, but the butterflies do not. They stream into the air, fluttering around the room as vibrantly as when they were alive, as if they'd never died and been pinned to backing boards.

I try to catch them with my hands, but they're too fast. I look from the mess on the floor to the bugs in the air, and I have no idea what to do.

I lift my hands to the air, tears flowing down my cheeks, and scream.

"Stop! Just stop!"

All at once, the butterfly bodies freeze and fall.

Dozens of butterflies lie on the ground, lifeless, surrounded by broken glass.

I slump to my knees, careful not to land on any sharp shards or delicate specimens. And there, casting green light in the middle of the shattered glass and crooked wings, is the stone. I wipe the tears from my face and pick it up, feeling its cold weight in my palm.

If I can't get rid of the stone, I have to do what Ingrid would do—what a real scientist would do.

I have to go next door and get some answers.

PART II
Question

Chapter 5

Supplies I always bring when conducting research in the field: a notebook, a flashlight, a compass, and a multitool. I also grab some granola bars for good measure.

A good scientist is always prepared.

The stone sits in my right pocket. Its chill seeps through the fabric of my jeans, a constant reminder of its presence. If I can't get rid of it, maybe it will protect me from whatever awaits next door.

The wrought iron fence between the Elm House and mine is overgrown with shrubs, but I remember the way Soren disappeared through here when I thought he was a cat. I investigate the bushes until I find a small, hidden gap. It's much too small for a grown-up to fit through, but it is just the right size for a cat, a lemur, or a girl like me.

I get on my hands and knees and crawl through, pushing branches away from my face. Two of the fence's bars are rusted and bent, making an opening that I can fit through. I emerge on the other side of the fence in another tangle of bushes. The plants on this side are covered in thorns, and some of them pull at the fabric of my clothes as I push through. I'm careful to avoid snagging my skin on them. Beyond the rosebushes is a neatly trimmed lawn leading to the main house.

I've lived next to the Elm House my entire life, but I've never seen it up close before. It always had a drab, gray look to it, with peeling paint and boarded-up windows. But now it looks fresh, as if it were just painted yesterday. It doesn't match the other houses in my neighborhood, with their tan paint and square roofs. This house is not as wide as the other houses, but it's taller, at least three stories. The highest window is in a round, narrow tower at the top. The entire house is painted in bright colors: yellow and orange and green. Carved white columns create a porch that wraps around the front. The house looks like it belongs to another place and time, like something out of a movie set.

To my right is the front gate, chained and locked, and a cobblestone path leading to the front door. Two birds splash in a marble birdbath in the center of the garden. There are perfectly shaped hedges lining the entirety of the yard and rosebushes lined up in neat rows. Little cards stick out of the dirt in front of each plant. I bend down to look at one marking a rosebush with deep pink blossoms: Reine des Violettes. Hybrid Perpetual. 1860.

The garden is so neat and orderly that I don't know if it's the work of an artist or a scientist.

But I don't have time to admire the garden. Hand in my pocket, I grip the stone. I'm on a mission. I need to stay focused.

I walk up the path to the front door. There's a gold knocker the shape of a dragon's head mounted on the front. The dragon's ruby eyes stare back at me. Before I lift my hand to the knocker, the door creaks open by itself.

"Um...hello?" My voice shakes more than a scientist's should. I clear my throat and step inside.

I don't know what I expected. Something dark and creepy, maybe, like a haunted house. Dusty couches and cobwebs and a piano that plays itself. But that's not what I find.

A crystal chandelier casts golden light around the entryway. The white walls are carved with swirling floral patterns and elaborate shapes. Intricately woven red-and-gold carpets cover the dark wooden floor. To the left, an archway leads into a room with high windows, and I can see the garden and the birdbath beyond them. To the right are two closed doors. A grand staircase straight ahead leads up.

At the top of the staircase is a gigantic portrait of an elegant woman and man, both dressed in black. The woman is standing, one hand on the man's shoulder, her hair pulled back into a loose, messy bun. Her blue eyes are sharp and determined, like she's challenging the viewer to a duel. The man looks more thoughtful, his hair combed and neatly parted to the side, his eyes looking away.

"Hello?" My voice echoes through the empty room, louder than before. There is no response.

My legs shake, but a scientist has to be brave. I take a step toward the staircase.

A gust of wind blows through the room, and the front door slams behind me. I spin around, but no one is there. Maybe this house *is* haunted. Heart pounding, I face the stairs again.

I'm no longer alone.

At the top of the steps stands a woman. Her brown hair is pulled into a messy bun at the top of her head—the same woman from the portrait. She wears a deep-purple shirt and loose black trousers that billow around her legs like a skirt. Golden honeybee earrings dangle from her ears. Beside her is Soren the lemur. He blinks his yellow eyes at me.

"Juniper Edwards." The woman's voice is commanding, her British accent slippery smooth. "I've been expecting you."

She descends the stairs, and I step back until I hit the front door. She stops in front of me, much taller than I am, and bends down to look at me with her piercing eyes. Then she holds one hand out, palm up.

"May I see it?"

My fingers still grip the stone in my pocket. I hesitate. What will she do to it? To me? All the "stranger danger" warnings from my parents flood into my mind. But I'm here for answers, and I suspect she has them. I lift the stone out of my pocket and place it in her palm. The green light dances in her eyes. She turns the stone over in her hands.

"Fascinating."

I feel that same magnetic feeling as I watch her examine the stone. I want to grab it, put it back in my pocket where it will be safe.

I shiver, and the feeling passes. I came here to learn about the stone, so it makes sense to show it to her. After a moment she places the stone back into my hand. I stick it quickly back into my pocket, but I don't let go.

"I know you are afraid." Her voice is quiet now, soothing. She puts a hand on my shoulder. "Things are happening to you that you don't understand. But I can help you understand them, if you'd like."

My eyes dart up to Soren, who is still perched at the top of the stairs. He nods. I look back at the woman.

"Who are you?"

She stands up straight with a flourish. The honeybees hanging from her ears sparkle.

"My name is Artemis Alderdice—scientist, magician, and natural philosopher. This house is my laboratory."

A scientist *and* a magician? Those two things don't make sense together. But nothing about this makes sense.

"I'm a scientist too," I say.

She grins and holds out a hand.

"Then come—I'll give you the grand tour and explain everything."

Artemis's boots echo across the hardwood floors as she leads me through the archway to the room overlooking the garden. It is called the parlor, she explains. It looks like a room from one of those old-timey British TV shows Mom watches, which she calls "period dramas." There's fancy carved wooden furniture, embroidered floral curtains, and a grand piano. But there are some things that you wouldn't find in one of those television manor houses. As we move from room to room, I notice antique scientific oddities—brass astrolabes, geocentric models of the solar system, and other mysterious outdated devices.

We go into a room that looks like another living room but smaller. Books fill wall-to-wall shelves, and there's a warm fire burning in the fireplace.

"This is the sitting room," Artemis says. I don't know the difference between a parlor and a sitting room. "I spend a lot of time reading in here. Any good magician is well-read."

"I thought you said you were a scientist?"

Artemis shrugs and picks up a book.

"Same thing. Magic and science are two sides of the same coin. Both are worthy of study."

"That's why I came here. To study…whatever this is."

"I think we'll work nicely together, you and I. Natural curiosity is a special trait. Come, I have more to show you."

She leads me out of the parlor and up the staircase. I pause in front of the giant painting on the landing.

"That's you, isn't it?"

Artemis stops and regards the painting, a strange, sad look in her eyes.

"A long, long time ago."

Once we're up the stairs, I try to slow down so I can better observe my surroundings. The walls in the upstairs hall are a soft cream color, and they're decorated elaborately, with torches mounted next to dozens of works of art. There are several closed doors, and I wonder what mysteries lie behind them. She points to the one at the very end.

"That's the bathroom, if you ever need it. But I know you're not here to see old-fashioned plumbing."

That's one mystery solved.

Artemis pulls out a large, ornate key and opens the first door a crack, then pauses.

"Before we go further...I want you to know that what I'm showing you requires the utmost secrecy. Do you understand?"

I nod. I have no one to tell about this. The only person who would understand is Ingrid—and she's gone.

"All right, then. Welcome to my laboratory."

She pushes the door open, and I gasp. This is not a typical lab. There are desks, tables, bookshelves, and even a couch, but every surface is covered with strange apparatuses, vials of mysteriously colored liquids, and piles of scrawled notes with strange symbols drawn on them. The books are old and have titles with words like *Alchemy* and *Magick*.

A terrarium on one of the desks catches my eye. Inside is a large moth, sitting upon a stick. On its hind wings are two large spots that look like eyes.

"Careful. That's not a normal moth."

"It's a Polyphemus moth," I say. "But…"

The spots blink. They don't just look like eyes. They *are* eyes. I stumble backward, and Artemis chuckles.

"A young entomologist, are you?"

"My parents are entomologists." This is something I've always been proud of, and now it will actually come in handy. "I am too. But I've never seen a moth do that."

"It's not a normal moth…and as you've probably surmised, I'm not a normal scientist. Come, sit. Let's have a chat."

She sits down on the velvet couch and pats the cushion beside her. Soren jumps up on the back of the couch and perches behind her head. I sit, pulling my backpack onto my lap. It feels like a protective barrier between me and this strange new world I've found myself in.

"Let's start with you." Her voice is gentle, but fear still twists my stomach. "Why did you come here today, Juniper?"

"I want to know what's happening to me. I want to know what all…*this* is." I gesture around the room. "You call it magic, but that can't be real. Magic isn't real."

I tell her about nearly drowning, and the way things look different. I tell her about what happened in English class, how things just started growing and I couldn't get them to stop. I tell her about the butterflies. She reaches over and holds my hand in hers, comfortingly. Her fingers are thin, bony, and cold, but I feel my shaking breath steady a little.

"I know it won't be easy for you to understand, Juniper, but I will try to explain as best I can. What's happening to you *is* magic."

"But magic isn't real," I protest.

Artemis sighs, then lifts my hand between us, face up. She covers it with her own, and when she moves her hand away, a white orb of light sits above my palm. It floats upward, like a bubble. I reach out to touch it, and when my fingertips meet its glowing edge, it pops into a tiny firework and dissipates into the air.

"How did you do that?"

"Magic," Artemis says. "If you truly are a scientist, Juniper, then you must try to have an open mind. I have been studying magic scientifically for a long time—I'm older than I look."

Could magic actually be real? My brain feels all jumbled. There must be a scientific explanation. Science holds the answer to everything. I have to trust the scientific method. I have to observe.

"Okay," I say. "I'll try."

"I have a theory about what's happening to you. When you fell into the water at the nature preserve, you experienced what I call a magical event."

I pull out my notebook and pencil and write *magical event*.

"A magical event is a seemingly random magical phenomenon. Events like these happen in various geographic locations around the world. I started studying magical events in England, and I followed them across the Atlantic, across the continent, all the way to this Los Angeles suburb. Magical events are common here."

I take careful notes as she speaks.

"Then this isn't the first time this has happened," I say.

"They don't always manifest the same way, but they have similar properties—objects infused with magical ability, inexplicable phenomena. I have various methods of tracking magical events that I've devised over the years. You see, I have this theory that there is another place, unreachable by normal humans, that I call the magical plane. And this magical plane sometimes touches ours—"

Soren clears his throat.

"Well, I'm getting ahead of myself," Artemis says, waving the thought away. "What's important is that one of these magical events happened to you."

"It was random, then." The idea that this happened to me by chance makes me feel better. Science and nature are filled with random occurrences, chance interactions. Life itself happened by chance, billions of years ago. I can understand that.

But Artemis hesitates.

"*Seemingly* random," she clarifies. "I don't have enough data to make that assumption."

"If the phenomenon is random, that means it's not repeatable." I sigh. "And if we can't repeat it, then we can't test it."

"Ah! That brings me to the second important bit." Artemis straightens, her entire face lighting up. She has the same look Mom gets when she gets to share some exciting historical trivia at the museum.

I ready my pencil again.

"Magical events aren't the only way to get magic," Artemis continues. "It can also be learned. Studied. After all, I never experienced my own magical event. I was taught. The abilities you've described would take years for someone to study and perfect. Decades. A lifetime."

She grabs my hands, and my pencil clatters to the floor. Her piercing eyes dig deep into mine.

"You have a great power, Juniper. Greater even than my own. You have life itself at your fingertips. If you learn to control it, you can do great things."

I look down at my hands. There are pencil smudges on my fingertips. It's hard to believe that they hold so much power.

"But how do I get it under control?" I ask. "I don't want things to grow around me all the time."

"Think like a scientist, Juniper. To control something, you

have to understand it. And to understand it, you have to observe it instead of trying to suppress it. Let your powers loose, and see what happens."

"And what then? Even if I can control them, what do I use them for?"

"What then, indeed." Artemis smiles at me. "That's something you have to decide for yourself. Though I dare say, it would be nice to have such a sharp lab assistant."

Artemis winks, and I feel a surge of pride and anticipation. *Lab assistant.* I have always wanted to do research, but magical research?

"I don't know..."

Artemis stands, crosses the room to one of the bookshelves, and pulls out a large, dusty book. She blows on the cover, specks of glittering dust floating in the beams of light. The title carved into the leather cover reads *Alchymy, Magicks, and Natural Philosophy*.

She hands it to me, and it's heavier than it looks. I run my fingers along the side, feeling the rough edges of the pages.

"Read that," Artemis says. "Experiment with your powers. Then return to me. Once you know more about the subject, you'll be able to make a more informed decision."

If I learn enough about magic, I can do real research. It would be magical science, but I bet I can find a way to spin it for future college applications. It would make Ingrid proud.

I tuck the book into my backpack with shaking hands, excitement beating out the fear. I practically skip as Artemis shows me out. But the excitement morphs into dread as I make my way back through the gap between our houses and hear my parents calling my name.

Chapter 6

I am in the biggest trouble I've ever been in my entire life.

I've always been the well-behaved child. When headstrong Ingrid picked fights with Dad, I always did as I was told. But ever since Ingrid died, everything I do is wrong.

The worst was when Chelsea and I got detention for fighting a month after Ingrid died. Chelsea told me I should smile more. I pulled on her dangly earring that was really just a whole pencil, eraser and all, hanging from her earlobe. Things devolved from there.

Mom and Dad were livid, and I had to do extra chores for a month. But they weren't nearly as upset as they are now.

I sit on the living room couch, covered in mud and grass stains. Mom sits next to me, squeezing my hand, as Dad paces around the room and examines the broken glass butterflies littering the floor.

"Where *were* you?" Mom asks. "The school said you ran away. I thought…"

"I'm sorry, Mom," I say. "School was really hard and…I panicked."

It's not a lie, not exactly, but I still feel guilty. Mom's eyes glisten.

"You've made some very poor choices," Dad says, raising his voice. "Very poor. Mrs. Cartwright told me what happened yesterday. Wandering away from the group, going off the path. I was going to let it go, but now ditching school!"

"It was an accident—"

"An accident!"

"Dave." Mom's voice is quiet and calm. Dad stops and lets out a breath that deflates him like a big balloon. He sinks into the couch next to me.

"Maybe you can explain what's going on," Mom says, rubbing my back.

I tell them that after running away from school, I sat in the bushes and wrote in my notebook. That's believable enough, even though it's a for-sure lie.

"And you didn't hear us calling for you?" she asks. She has a deep, concerned crease between her eyebrows. I look down at my muddy fingers.

"I was distracted."

We sit in silence. I don't know if they believe my lie, but I know they wouldn't believe the truth, either.

"Dad and I are going to talk about this," Mom says finally. "This is obviously very…concerning behavior. Why don't you go upstairs and get cleaned up?"

I know what kind of conversation they're going to have now. It's the same one they've had before, about grief counseling and what they could've done differently to stop this from happening. They hug me and I head upstairs, feeling like a scolded dog. I can't wallow too long, though—there are more important things to do.

I pull the book Artemis gave me out of my backpack. It's very heavy, heavier than any other books I have, even my *Jepson Manual*. I set it on my desk with a *thunk* and stare at it. "Old" is an understatement. This book is ancient. The cover might have been red once, but it's faded to a dusty orange. The rough edges of the pages are worn down from centuries of use.

The answers to all my questions are inside this old, dusty book. I desperately want to know its secrets, but I hesitate. Will it fall apart if I open it? Should I wear gloves? I don't know anything about old books—that's probably Mateo's specialty—but Artemis gave it to me, so it must not be too fragile. I take a deep breath and open the front cover.

The yellowed and stained title page is adorned with elaborate black illustrations. In one corner, a lizard engulfed in flames sits above the word *Fire*. In another corner, a flock of birds among a large cloud represents *Air*. In the other two corners, a menagerie of monkeys, cows, squirrels, and elephants sit above the word *Earth*, and great sea serpents erupting from the ocean represent *Water*.

In the center of them all, surrounded by dark black ink, are jumbled images of moons and stars, goats and bears and centaurs. I squint down at the drawings and realize they are depicting the constellations. Written beneath is the word *Chaos*.

The title is below in an elegant script: *Alchymy, Magicks, and Natural Philosophy*. Under that: *1658*. This book is nearly four hundred years old.

A knock startles me. I shut the book and shove it into my desk drawer just as Mom cracks the door open.

"Hey, June," she says. "I was just talking to Dad."

She sits on my bed and pats the space next to her. I flop down, and she puts an arm around me.

"Am I in trouble?"

"Not exactly," she says gently. "But maybe going to school today was a mistake, after what happened yesterday."

I shrug. "I feel okay."

"It's not just how your body feels," she says. "Having an experience like that can be emotionally taxing on a person."

"I don't feel 'emotionally taxed.'"

She places a hand over mine. "Did someone bother you at school?"

"Not really." I look down at my feet. A silence stretches between us. I have no way to tell her the truth. How am I supposed to explain my newfound magic powers? I can't. So I don't say anything at all.

"Dad and I decided that you should stay home the rest of the week. You need time to recover. We'll take turns off work, so you won't be home alone."

"I don't want to stay home," I say. "What about the poetry test?"

Mom gives me a knowing look. She's well aware that poetry is not my best subject.

"I'll email Mr. Harris and see if he can give you a make-up test once you're back."

I don't like the idea of being stuck in the house with my parents. How am I supposed to study magic with them observing my every move? But maybe this is good—at least if I stay home for a few days, I'll have plenty of time to read.

Mom pulls me into a big hug.

"I know things are hard," she says over my shoulder, "but we're here for you. We're always here for you. We love you so much. Don't be too hard on yourself."

I know she loves me, but I don't think she'll ever understand why I push so hard. I can't tell her about magic, just like I can't tell her about hunting the Blue. She'll tell me to let it go, to focus on other things. But I can't let it go. Not catching the Blue is a betrayal to Ingrid, and letting magic go unexplained is a betrayal to science.

"I love you too, Mom."

She pulls away and squeezes my hand.

"I'm making pasta, so come down in a few minutes, okay?"

I wait on my bed until she closes the door behind her. I'm not in that much trouble, after all. When I go down for dinner it feels almost normal—Mom talks about some annoying tourists she got to kick out of the museum, and Dad recounts an interesting conversation he had with his coworker about rare African pill bugs. We don't talk about anything that happened. After dinner they ask if I want to watch a movie, but I tell them I'm too tired and slip up to my room.

I pull the book out of my desk drawer, along with my notebook. I have work to do.

One time Mom took us to a museum that had very old books on display. All of them were carefully arranged on book stands, propped open, and the curators had to turn the pages every few days so they wouldn't fade under the museum lights.

Sitting with this ancient book open before me, I feel like a museum curator carefully turning the pages. It's hard to decipher because many of the words are spelled differently than in modern English. Even more confusing, sometimes the letter *s* looks like the letter *f*.

A few pages into the introduction is a section underlined in blue ink, so I skip ahead to read that part:

Magick is natural; which all excellent wife men do admit and embrace, and worfhip with great applaufe; neither is there anything more highly efteemed, or better thought of, by men of learning. The moft noble Philofophers that ever were, greate Magicians and Alchymyfts, alter the World with the force of their own defire. This Magickal energy is thus focufed through a specific Magick item of their choofing.

A magic item. I pull the stone out of my pocket and set it next to the book. Green light washes over my desk, filling the room with an eerie glow.

If this stone is my magic item, that would make me a magician.

I turn back to the book. Next to the underlined text, in matching blue ink, someone has written:

OR ENERGY FROM THE MAGICAL PLANE IMBUES THE MAGICIAN.

Artemis said something about her theory of a magical plane. Did she write these notes? The ink looks brighter, fresher than the decaying yellow pages of the book.

There's no way I'll be able to read this entire book in one night. The text is small, and the author drones on about things that aren't magical at all. There are sections on distilling salt water that I know are scientific facts, no magic needed. There are long passages about fruit preservation and household management that I skip.

I pay particular attention to anything underlined in blue, even if some of the claims are questionable. The kind of science in this book is very different from the science I've learned to love. The scientific method is nonexistent here. *This* science comes from the heart. Experiments can go awry, it claims, if the practitioner has too weak a will, or too much bile in their blood, whatever that means.

But the science it describes holds endless possibility to alter the world. Alchemists can turn lead into gold with the right conditions and intentions, or magicians can change their appearance and become shapeshifters. According to the book, it doesn't even take special powers; anyone can learn the secrets of the universe and bend it to their will.

Logically, I know that all of this is outdated nonsense. But then again…my eyes drift to the glowing green stone on my desk. I've seen for myself what magic can do. Who's to say the other things in this book aren't real?

My eyes start to feel sticky as I read a long recipe for turning tin to silver in a chapter titled "Of Changing Metals." There's no way I could actually try it—I'd have to melt tin over a fire for several days and then add vinegar. I don't even know where to get tin, and I definitely don't have several days to heat it.

Maybe I'm reading the wrong sections. I flip to the front of the book and look at the table of contents. I skim over the chapters about changing metals, distillation, and cookery, but stop on the last one: "Of the Chaos."

I heft the pages over until I find the final chapter. The other chapters were filled with practical diagrams and illustrations of plants. But this one is different. On the first page is an illustration of a girl, lying on her back, floating in the air. Golden hair spills from her head, and standing behind her is a man in a black cloak, raising his arms. His face is smudged out.

The Chaos, wherein the Experiments set within are ineffable and go beyond what is known to mankinde of the Natural Sciences.

I think of the way sprouts cracked through the surface of my desk, and the butterfly wings that circled my living room. I think of talking lemurs and a house that looks abandoned one day and pristine the next. These are not things I would consider scientific. But at the time this book was written, things like making jam and distilling water seemed more like magic. Maybe the book, despite being so old, is right. Maybe these magical things *are* science—we just don't understand it yet.

The contents are as grim as the picture. This page—no, I realize, flipping ahead, the next dozen pages—are about life and death. The blue ink underlines and annotates throughout.

Bringing forth the Dead is akin to the leavening of Bread, a confluence of the Elements and the greate desire of all things for Life.

I read until my head aches, gulping down the words as fast as I can, realizations clicking into place.

Roots sprouting from long-dead wood. Butterflies pulling themselves up from their pins. The magic doesn't just make things grow.

I made dead things come back to life.

It's five in the morning by the time I crawl into bed, the stone clutched tightly in my hand. I turn it over in my fingers under the blanket. I toss and turn, but I can't fall asleep, even as thin beams of morning light filter through my window. I see the smudged face of the man behind my eyelids. *Life and death.* The seed of a hypothesis sprouts in my mind.

Chapter 7

When I wake up, the sun is already high in the sky. Mom is long gone to work, and Dad is in the den, fixing the mess I made. He sits at the big desk, straightening the specimens before slipping them into a new frame.

"Morning, Dad."

He sets down his tweezers and looks up at me.

"Morning, sleepyhead," he says cheerfully. "It's past noon."

I look at the clock above the fireplace. He's right. I stayed up much later than I meant to, and I'm still tired. I slump down on the couch and yawn.

"I was up kind of late last night. Reading."

"Well, you can sleep all day if you want." He pushes his glasses up the bridge of his nose and picks up the tweezers again, turning back to the bugs. "Oh, and I'm making beef stroganoff for dinner."

Dad knows his beef stroganoff is one of my favorite foods. I haven't eaten much since I fell. If this is a ploy to get me to eat more, it's working.

"Do you think you'll be okay by yourself if I run to the store for the ingredients?"

"I'll be fine," I say. "I might sit in the backyard. For some fresh air."

"Just don't wander off." He says it playfully, but there's an edge to his voice.

"I won't. Promise."

I get dressed and run back downstairs just as Dad puts his keys and wallet in his pocket.

"I'll be back in half an hour," he says. "Stay out of trouble."

"I will."

I watch by the window until his car disappears around the block. Then I run down the hall and into the living room.

Dad's desk is littered with tweezers, pins, and specimens from his unfinished repinning project. I find what I'm looking for: a specimen with olive-green-and-copper wings. *Callophrys gryneus*, the Juniper Hairstreak. I lift it carefully. What better butterfly to experiment on than the one I'm named after?

I carry it cupped in my palms to the backyard.

My backyard is nothing special. It's just a concrete patio with a pile of sun-bleached sand toys and several pots of tomato cages, the plants within long dead. A patchy rectangle of grass is surrounded on all sides by brick walls, lined with bushes in various states of dead and not dead.

I stand in the center of the patchy lawn, unsure of what I should do, exactly. Dad isn't home, but what if a neighbor peeks over the wall and sees me? *Stop it*. I know I'm being paranoid. I take a deep breath and remember what Artemis said. In order to control my power, I have to observe it.

I hold my hands out in front of me. The gossamer wings of the Juniper Hairstreak sit lifelessly on my fingers. The book said that magic flows from the magician. The notes in the margins said it comes from a magical plane. I don't know which is right, but I close my eyes, imagining the magic flowing all around the butterfly. I remember the way the butterflies pulled themselves from the backing board, the pins dropping as their wings sprang to life. Wind rustles strands of my hair against my cheek.

I open my eyes, but the butterfly hasn't moved.

I huff and reach into my pocket. Maybe the stone is the key. I hold the stone next to the butterfly, its green light washing over the wings. I hold my breath…

Nothing happens.

The magic book said nothing about how to make the magic *go*. It talked about strong will and something about divine intervention, but not how to turn the magic on. What am I doing wrong?

I pace around the backyard, the stone gripped in one hand

and the butterfly carefully cupped in the other. Yesterday, the magic flowed out of me uncontrollably. Today, it's gone. There's something I'm missing—some element I need to make the magic work. I think back to English class. What was different?

I was inside, not outside. I was around a lot of people, not alone. I was sitting, not standing. I was holding a pencil, not a butterfly. But there's no way to know if these factors show causation or correlation—a scientist's way of saying a result has a cause or is just coincidence. There are too many unknowns with magic. When scientists want to test something, they usually do a control experiment first, so they can compare the tests to that. But I don't have a control experiment—all I have is chaos. How am I supposed to test my new powers if I have nothing to compare them to?

My heart thuds impatiently. I'm running out of time. Dad will be back any minute. This has to work.

I close my eyes again and squeeze every muscle in my body. My fingers grip the stone so tight my fingernails bite into my palm. *Please*, I beg. *Make something happen.*

But when I open my eyes, the butterfly is motionless.

I throw the stone across the yard, and it hits the brick wall. What was the point of staying up all night to study magic if I can't even test it? All the hope and excitement I felt evaporates. I'm out of time.

Maybe it was a fluke. Maybe Artemis is wrong, and I don't have magic after all. Maybe I've been in a coma since I fell into the creek, and this is all an elaborate dream.

I turn back toward my house, but my foot catches on something and I fall. I land hard on my elbows, careful not to crush the Juniper Hairstreak. I try to stand, but my foot is stuck. I look behind me.

A vine snakes its way around my ankle. I didn't feel it slither over my jeans. I try to pull my leg free, but its grip tightens. I set the Juniper Hairstreak down gently on the grass before rolling over. The grass is growing at an alarming rate, the tips of the blades tickling my arms as I try to pull the vine off my ankle. But as soon as I rip part of the vine off, another sprouts up and replaces it. Dozens of shoots emerge all around me, grabbing at my ankles, my knees, my arms. Thick tendrils wrap around my elbows, and I lose my grip as they wrench my hands away. Panic wells up in my throat—this isn't what I wanted to happen.

The vines wrap around my waist, my legs, my chest, until I'm lifted off the ground. I struggle desperately, but their hold tightens. I feel them slide along the skin of my neck, pressing against my throat. Soon I won't be able to breathe.

Out of the corner of my eye I see a flash of gray fur and yellow eyes.

"Soren—help—" I try to call out to him, but the vines strangle me.

This is it. This is how I'm going to die—asphyxiated by my own uncontrollable magic.

The vines slide around my head. I feel their cold, crisp flesh against my cheeks. One works its way around my temple, dangerously close to my eyes.

Green-and-copper wings flutter against the blue sky before my eyes are covered. Everything goes dark.

"Juniper!"

The familiar voice sounds distant. My ears thunder with the creaking and cracking of the vines and the pounding of my own heartbeat. There's a blast of icy air, strange for a sunny California day. The vines' grip loosens, and I struggle again, kicking against the crush of plants as hard as I can. Another blast of cold, moist air hits me, saturating my hair and clothes with icy water. The vines let go suddenly, and I fall to the ground on a plush bed of foot-long grass.

I lie there for a moment, shivering and gasping for air. A dark shape stands above me, blocking out the sun with a mass of curly brown hair.

"Mateo?" I choke, my throat sore from the grip the vines had on my neck.

Mateo's cheeks are red, and his jeans and T-shirt are soaked. He's holding the garden hose, water dribbling slowly from the spout. He tosses it to the side and reaches out a hand.

I take it, feeling the bite of ice against my skin. His hands are freezing. Little bits of ice drip off his skin. I let him help me sit up. My head spins as I look around my backyard. A few minutes ago it was filled with half-dead plants. Now it's green and overgrown. The strangling vines have disappeared, but evidence of the magic lingers. The grass is long and wavers in the gentle breeze. Bright red blooms weigh heavily on the previously neglected rose bushes. Even the tomato cages are filled with plump, red tomatoes. Mateo crouches in front of me.

"Are you all right?" he asks.

"What are you doing here?" I counter, ignoring the question. I don't know if I'm all right.

"No one answered the door," he explains. "I heard shouting, so I hopped the fence."

"I don't need you checking in on me," I say.

He winces. Bright red blood oozes through a tear in his jeans.

"You're hurt!"

"I'll be okay," he says. "And if I hadn't been here, those vines might've killed you."

"I had it under control."

He gives me a skeptical look.

"Sure you did," he says. He pauses for a moment, looking away. "Magic is very difficult to control."

The words sit between us for several seconds. *Magic*. I look at the melting ice dripping off Mateo's skin, glistening in the warm sun. That ice didn't come out of my hose. It must have come out of *him*.

"What do you know about magic?" I ask, trying not to sound too excited.

"I know that it causes more problems than it solves." He chews on his lip. "I saw what happened to you in class yesterday.

You haven't had magic long, have you?"

"No," I say, staring at his hands. He catches me looking and shoves them in his pockets. "Have you?"

"I don't do magic. Not anymore."

"You did it just now to save me, didn't you? You know how to do magic!" The words tumble out as my mind races with new possibilities. Artemis and Soren aren't the only magicians.

"Only because I had to," Mateo says. "Nothing good can come out of using magic. Trust me."

I open my mouth to argue, but I stop myself. Covered in dirt and almost strangled by vines, I'm not exactly a shining example of good magic. Besides, maybe this could be an opportunity. Mateo might be a nosy, annoying boy who doesn't know how to mind his own business—but he has *magic*. A good scientist collects data from as many sources as possible, and a new source just presented itself. I push myself up and attempt to wipe the grass stains from my clothes.

"Will you tell me about magic, at least?" I ask.

"No," he says, shaking his head. "No, I—I can't. I told you I don't do magic anymore."

"Please?" I try my best to sound nice, not desperate. "I just want to know what's happening to me. Like you said, I almost died because I don't know what I'm doing."

Mateo backs away, shaking his head. He looks stricken, his eyes wide. *Scared.*

"I promise I won't do anything irresponsible," I say quickly.

"But what if it tries to kill me again? You won't always be here."

He chews on his lip again.

"I don't do magic anymore," he repeats. But it sounds more like he's trying to convince himself, not me.

I glance at my back door. Dad will be home any minute and I'm starting to get impatient.

"I have magic now, Mateo," I say. "And I can't get rid of it, so I'm going to study it, whether you help me or not. And if you don't help me, something bad could happen, like you said. So are you going to help me, or are you going to let me die?"

It's dramatic, but Mateo likes poetry, so he must like drama. And it works.

"Okay," he says finally. "I can teach you some things. Just enough so you can get it under control. But nothing else. Okay?"

"Deal," I say. "But you need to go. My dad will be mad if he finds us back here like this."

I start trudging through the tall grass to the side gate.

"I can come by tomorrow, after school," Mateo says.

"That works," I say as I unlatch the gate for him. "I'll see you tomorrow."

I watch Mateo walk down the driveway and onto the side-walk. Just as he disappears from view, Dad's car trundles up the street and pulls into the driveway. I quickly shut the gate and run back into the house and up the stairs. Once I'm in my room, I shove my grass-stained clothes as far into the hamper as they'll go.

PART III
Hypothesize

Chapter 8

The next morning I wake up early. Mom is using her unexpected day off to sleep in. I want to go see Artemis, but I'll need to think of a way to get away from Mom for a couple hours, and that's not an easy thing to do.

I bring the magic book downstairs to the living room to read while I wait for Mom to wake up. I'm better at deciphering the outdated language now. I skip around to the passages underlined in blue.

Certaine Elements of the body are not difficult to retrieve, but that which makes the Soul is not so easily shewn.

The coffee grinder whirs to life in the kitchen, and I know

Mom is awake. I shove the book behind one of the couch cushions. Mom sits next to me and puts an arm around my shoulders, blowing on the steaming liquid in her mug.

"It's nice having a day off," she says. "What do you want to do today?"

I shrug. I can't tell her what I *really* want to do today.

"We could go out for Froyo," she says, drawing out the syllables.

"For breakfast?" I ask, surprised. Froyo is my weakness.

"Why not?"

We race to get dressed, like we used to do when I was small, and get into the car. I can figure out visiting Artemis later. The novelty of getting Froyo on a weekday morning with Mom almost makes me forget about magic. Mom isn't strict—but being academics, my parents are "process oriented," as they describe it. They like routine. It's fun seeing Mom wear jeans and eat gummy worms when she's supposed to be at work and I'm supposed to be at school.

I feel lighter on the way home. We laugh about the ridiculous commercials on the radio. Mom glances at me out of the corner of her eye as she drives, smiling wide. When she first told me she'd be staying home, I thought it was a burden for her to miss work at the museum. But I can tell she's having fun.

My smile fades when we turn onto our street and the Elm House comes into view. I don't see any lights on, but I imagine Artemis standing in the highest window, watching me from above. Maybe Soren's lounging on the wall between our houses, tail flicking curiously. I look back to Mom. She's still smiling, still happy. It reminds me of the good times when Ingrid was alive. But I can't be happy when I know there's a heaviness that weighs on Mom's heart that will never go away. That weighs on all our hearts. How can I smile while Ingrid rots in a grave?

When we get inside, Mom's cell phone rings.

"It's Grandma," she says.

Whenever Grandma calls, she talks Mom's ear off for an hour at least. This is my chance.

"I'm going to lie down," I say. "I think I ate too much Froyo."

Mom nods as she answers the call. I run upstairs and shut my bedroom door.

I've never snuck out of my room, but I know it can be done. Ingrid and our older cousin did it a few years ago, but I was too afraid to do it then. I stayed inside and watched them climb out onto the eaves and jump down to the brick wall. Now I throw open the window. I know Mom will be disappointed if she finds out, but I can't wait any longer. I tuck the book into my backpack, take a deep breath, and climb through the window.

I've never considered myself afraid of heights, but up here on the roof my head sways. I crouch down, my fingers fumbling at the red-brown terra-cotta tiles, but there's not a way to get a firm grip. I shimmy down the roof on my bottom until I get to the edge. The wall is only about two feet away, but it feels much farther. I let out a breath, then jump.

I grab the top of the wall, legs dangling below me, but I can't hold on for long. I let go and land on my feet, the shock of the concrete reverberating into my legs. My body is sore and shaking with nerves, but I made it. I look up at my open window, the thin curtain fluttering in the breeze. I didn't make a plan for getting back in, but I'll worry about that later.

I dash across my driveway to the bushes. When I emerge on the other side of the fence, Soren is waiting for me. He stands on his hind legs, looking more human than lemur.

"A daring escape, if I do say so myself."

My face heats up. "Um, thank you."

"You made some improvements to your backyard yesterday," he says. "As a gardener myself, I recommend giving the tomatoes more direct sun."

"It's hard to imagine a lemur as a gardener."

"I was a gardener long before I was a lemur." He gestures to the roses. "In fact, this entire garden is my handiwork."

The garden is so peaceful. I can't hear the cars from the main highway or music bumping from nearby houses. It's like I've been transported to another world. "It's lovely."

Soren flicks his tail back and forth with an uncanny, human-like smile. His wide, yellow eyes look pleased at the compliment.

"It's easier with small hands," he says, holding up his small, black palms. "Come. I'll show you around."

I follow Soren across the lawn, around the stone fountain birdbath and toward the back of the house. He shows me the roses and the topiaries—bushes cut like statues. The garden is much bigger than I expected, filled with hedges and stepping stones and fountains. It seems to go on forever.

"Did you make this all on your own? It's extraordinary."

Soren responds with a poem:

> *Mary, Mary, quite contrary,*
> *How does your garden grow?*
> *With silver bells and cockle shells*
> *And pretty maids all in a row.*

Soren scampers across the path, his small feet kicking up brown pebbles as he goes.

"I was the youngest of nine children, and I spent most of my time outside with the plants instead of making friends. My siblings would tease me with that song."

"And they called you Mary?"

"A lot of people thought I was a girl back then," Soren says, shrugging. "Ironically, people are more willing to accept my lemur form than accept that I'm a man."

Soren leads me down the path toward an archway carved in a hedge. It leads to a kitchen garden at the back of the house, with planters of herbs and vegetables. "Some people use magic to amass great power and shape the world to their will. Me? I garden."

The back door opens, and Artemis emerges onto the porch.

She gazes at me through round goggles with a dozen different lenses on metal arms. They make her eyes look wide and bulging.

"You're back," she says. "I've been waiting for you."

Artemis's laboratory is small and cluttered but has an organized sort of chaos. I sit on the small couch, my backpack beside me, as Artemis bounces from table to table. There are bottles of strange liquids everywhere—shimmering golds and fluorescent blues. A strong chemical smell fills the air, but I don't recognize what it is.

"What are you making?" I ask.

"Potions!" Artemis exclaims.

"More like snake oil," Soren says. I hadn't noticed him perched in the window.

"Do be quiet, dear," Artemis says testily as she adjusts a small scale. "This is how I make a living—small spells and potions. Even magicians have bills, you know."

Artemis moves to another table. She picks up a beaker in one hand and uses an eyedropper to drip a yellow liquid into it. It sizzles when it mixes with the blue liquid within.

"I told you not to come back until you finished the book," Artemis says.

"I did finish it," I say, slipping the book and my notebook out of my backpack. I had spent another sleepless night poring over the text, especially the parts underlined in blue ink. "Well, most of it. I may have skimmed. But I paid attention to all the annotated parts. I took notes too."

"Ah, yes," Artemis says, lighting a Bunsen burner. "Those are the handiwork of a previous apprentice of mine. Her name was Ruby."

Ruby. Now I have a name to put to the notes.

"I think some of her notes were more useful than the book itself."

Artemis smiles wide at that, looking up at me. "Ruby was extremely clever. I still miss her terribly."

"What happened to her?" I ask.

Artemis turns back to the beaker. "She was lost," she says simply. "A long time ago."

There is only the sound of boiling liquid and the beat of my own heart in my chest. Artemis is quiet as she stirs the concoction over the flame.

"I lost my sister too," I say. "She loved science. More than me, even. I don't know if she'd understand all this magic stuff, but I think she'd find it fascinating. To study, I mean."

"It's a difficult thing, losing," she says.

I stare down at my hands. Ingrid wouldn't have believed in magic, but I know she would've wanted to study what was happening, to find whatever scientific explanation there was for it happening. She wouldn't settle for the book's idea that it was done with the power of the magician's own will. She'd put every overgrown plant, every reanimated insect under a microscope until she figured out the cause. She would try to replicate it, and she would take thorough notes. She would be a much better scientist about all this than me.

"I wish she was here," I whisper, more to myself than to Artemis.

For the first time since I arrived, Artemis stops. She sighs and leans against one of the tables, propping her strange goggles up onto her forehead.

"She sounds like she was a brilliant young woman," Artemis says. "I'm sure your own studies will make her proud."

I swallow the lump in my throat and nod.

"I hope so."

Artemis turns off the Bunsen burner and pulls off her gloves.

"Let's talk about science," she says. "Soren tells me you conducted some experiments of your own yesterday. How did that go?"

"Not great," I admit, glancing at Soren in the window. I tell her about the uncontrollable vines that almost smothered me. But I leave out the part about Mateo saving me—I don't know if Soren saw that part. It doesn't seem right to tell Artemis about Mateo. The fact that he has magic is his secret, not mine. And some selfish part of me wants to keep Artemis, Soren, and this magical house to myself.

"I managed to break free," I finish instead. I watch Artemis's face to see if she's caught me in the lie, but she simply nods. Her eyes are bright, excited.

"You hold a great power within you, Juniper," she says. "You understand now how science and magic are not so different. As there are endless possibilities with science, so too does magic have that same unlimited quality. I want to help you grow your power and use your skills for research."

"What sort of research?" I ask. "Potions?"

"Potions pay the bills, but the magical plane has always been the focus of my research," she says. "Ruby helped me with many of those experiments, but it's been a long time since I've dedicated time to its study. But now that the universe has placed such a powerful young apprentice into my living room, I think it's high time we take up some of those experiments again."

Soren sits up on his haunches and coughs in a startlingly humanlike way.

"Are you sure that's wise?" he asks.

"I know a lot about science too," I say, before Artemis changes her mind. "About conducting experiments and taking observational notes. I can be helpful!"

Artemis tips her head to one side, strands of curly hair escaping her bun and brushing against her shoulders.

"You have excellent enthusiasm," she says. "Let's see…"

She starts to pace around the room, counting on her fingers.

"If we're studying the magical plane, then I'll need that book, those notes…no, *those* notes burned in the fire…"

"Artemis." Soren's face is calm, but there's a hint of warning to his voice. Artemis ignores him.

"But perhaps I still have Ruby's...yes, and I still have all the vessels..." She walks back and forth, talking more to herself than to me or Soren.

"Artemis!"

She looks up then, as if just noticing he was there.

"I hear her mother calling," Soren says.

I turn toward the window, hearing the faint sound of my mother's voice shouting my name.

"I have to go." I shove the book and the notebook back into my backpack and dash out of the room. Artemis is right behind me, and she grabs my wrist.

"You are very powerful, Juniper," Artemis says. "Together, we will accomplish great things."

I nod, unsure of what to say. I slip my wrist out of her grasp and run down the stairs.

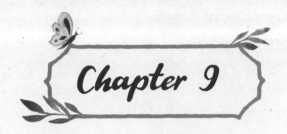

Chapter 9

Soren follows beside me, but he doesn't slink in his usual easy, comfortable way. He seems stiffer.

"Be careful, Juniper."

"I'm fine," I say. "I'll come up with some excuse—"

"No, not with your mother. I worry about how quickly Artemis is bringing you into her experiments. She can be hasty, obsessive—"

"It's going to be fine," I say again.

"Magical research of this nature is dangerous, Juniper. What do you hope to gain?"

He stops abruptly. I freeze. I've reached my own yard, but I'm not alone. Blinking down at me with wide brown eyes from the driveway is Mateo.

"Juniper? Why are you in the bushes?"

It can't be the afternoon already, can it? I lost track of time at the Elm House. I stand up and dust the soil off my knees. Something scratches at my ear, and I pull a twig out of my hair. I can't tell Mateo about Artemis and the magic house. If I do, he won't want to help me with magic. I say the first excuse I can think of.

"I, uh, saw a cool spirobolida."

He wrinkles his forehead as if I spoke a different language.

"Round-backed millipede," I say. It's a lie, but at least they're indigenous to the area. I helped Dad find some for his class once.

Mateo holds a folder and a rolled-up poster in his hands. "What's all that?"

"I brought your homework." He looks past me at the bushes. "Is someone there?"

I look back. Soren is gone—he probably scampered back through the fence when he saw Mateo.

"Nope."

"I heard you talking."

"I was talking to the millipedes."

Mateo laughs, but I didn't mean it to be funny. It was the first thing I thought of. Thankfully, Mateo doesn't push it. But his eyes still look behind me.

"That's a cool house," he says. "I never noticed it before."

I bite my lip. If I tell Mateo about the house next door, he'll know that there are others teaching me magic, and then he won't share what he knows. I have to keep Artemis and Soren a secret.

90

Besides, I swore I wouldn't tell anyone about them. Mateo might know about magic, but that doesn't mean I need to tell him everything.

"It's really old. My mom says it's a historic landmark." Not a lie.

"I wonder what kind of person lives in a house like that." Mateo's eyes look distant, the same way they looked when he was writing poetry on the bus.

"Maybe you can write a poem about it."

Mateo's eyes meet mine.

"Do you know them? Whoever lives there?"

The front door of my house opens, saving me from answering. Mom is not smiling like she was this morning. Her hair is a mess, and she looks frazzled.

"Juniper! There you are! I was so worried!" Her eyes land on Mateo. "Oh—hello."

"Mateo brought me my homework from school." I hold up the folder, and then I look at the poster. "What's this?"

"Oh, that's from Chelsea," Mateo explains. "She said it's your science project that's due on Monday. She did her part, so she said to just do your half and bring it back."

I tuck the rolled-up poster under my arm. I'd completely forgotten about the science project.

"Juniper, where were you?" There's a panicked hitch in Mom's voice.

Mateo looks at his feet.

"I came outside when I saw Mateo coming." The lie twists uncomfortably in my stomach. Mom looks so worried.

"I looked everywhere for you in the house." She leans against the doorframe, looking exhausted.

"I'm sorry," I say. The words hang heavily between the three of us. "Um, I was wondering, could I maybe go to Mateo's house to work on my homework?"

Mom looks between me and Mateo, a wrinkle between her eyebrows. The longer she thinks about it, the deeper the wrinkle gets.

"I live on the same street," Mateo says helpfully, pointing down the road. "Just around the corner."

"I'll be back before dinner," I add.

"I don't know…" Mom says. "I'll have to ask Dad."

"Mateo has the highest grade in English in the whole class," I say, pleading. "He promised to help me catch up."

Mateo nods. "We have a poetry project coming up," he says. "We have to write a poem."

My head snaps to him. "We have to *write* a poem? Mom, please. If Mateo doesn't help me, I'll definitely fail. You know how I am with poetry."

Mom lets out a big sigh, and then, surprisingly, she smiles.

"All right, all right, you wore me down," she says. "But don't go anywhere else, and be back before dinner. I'll text Dad about it."

I thank Mom profusely and run upstairs to grab my things. I leave the poster in my room, but I grab my English book, since

I told Mom that's what we'd be working on. I also put the magic book back into my desk drawer. Mateo will wonder where I got it, so I have to keep that a secret too. I do my best to scrape the mud off my clothes before running back downstairs. Mom stops me in the hallway.

"I'm glad to see you made a new friend, Juniper," she says. "Really glad."

I want to say "he's not my friend," but I stop myself. Is he my friend? We share secrets, but I'm not sure that's enough. I can think about it later—for now, Mom looks so happy that I don't want to ruin it for her.

Instead I say, "Be back in a bit!" and run out the door.

Mateo's house is at the end of my street. It was built in the same tract of houses as mine, so it looks a lot like mine, with the same windows and same color roof, but the rooms are arranged a little differently. His house is bright yellow, with scalloped white gables lining the rain gutters.

Mateo unlocks the door and leads me inside. The house smells like flowers. There are fresh flowers in vases all over and a lot of other knickknacks too. There are small statuettes of animals arranged neatly in a field of family photos on the mantle.

A woman appears through the kitchen door, with short curly hair like Mateo's that's gone a little silver. She has bottlecap glasses and a flowered apron.

"This is my tía Barbara," Mateo says.

Tía Barbara smiles wide, the skin around her eyes crinkling. She wipes her hands on her apron and puts one on my shoulder.

"Ah, Juniper! So you're the butterfly girl Mateo's told me about," she says, squeezing. "Are you hungry? I could make sandwiches."

"We've got homework, Tía," Mateo says.

"Well, I'll bring up some snacks in a bit," she says, patting my back. "It's wonderful to meet you, Juniper."

Mateo leads me up the stairs. There are photos on the walls of different people—baseball portraits, graduation photos, wedding pictures. How big is Mateo's family?

"Are your parents home?" I ask.

Mateo pauses, hand hovering over the doorknob.

"Oh, um. No. I live here with my aunt."

"Oh."

He pushes open the door, and my heart feels like it's fallen into my stomach. Does he mean his parents are gone?

I follow Mateo into his room, closing the door behind us. His room is not at all what I imagined. I thought of Mateo as a disorganized person, but the opposite is true. His room is extremely clean. The bed in the corner is made up, and all the papers on his desk are in a neat stack. Each pen and pencil has a place. The walls of his room are pale blue. There's a bookcase filled with books, but most of them are library books. Unlike my room, there are no clothes on the floor or posters on the walls. There's just one small picture taped to the wall by his bed. I recognize a younger Mateo, already with a big mop of hair, standing with a man and a woman in front of the ocean. They're all smiling from ear to ear.

"Haven't gotten around to decorating yet?" I ask.

"Hm?" Mateo looks around, as if he just noticed his walls for the first time. "Oh. Well, I don't know how long I'll be staying."

Mateo just moved here a couple months ago. That's when he started school, in the middle of the year. Would he move again already?

"Do you move around a lot?"

"It's hard to say," he says. "I lived in Seattle my whole life until I moved here."

"Did your parents get new jobs or something?" I ask.

"No, they're still in Seattle." Mateo looks down at his hands. "It's kind of a long story. I'm just…staying with my aunt Barbara for a while."

I'm glad Mateo's parents aren't dead. But I don't ask him any more questions. An awkward silence stretches between us.

Mateo sets his backpack down on his desk chair and sits cross-legged on the floor. I sit down across from him, plopping my own backpack down beside me.

"Anyway," he says, lifting his brown eyes to meet mine. "Magic."

"Magic," I repeat. I reach into my pocket and pull out the

stone. I set it on the floor between us.

Mateo's eyes go wide, his face illuminated with green light.

"Whoa." He leans in close to look at it from all directions, even pressing his cheek against the dark-blue carpet to get a better look without touching it. "I've never seen anything like this before."

"But I thought you do magic?" I ask. "Don't you have any sort of magic item?"

He glances toward his backpack.

"It's not exactly the same," he says. "It doesn't glow like yours does."

"Will you show me?"

Mateo rocks from side to side, considering. Finally, he unzips his backpack and pulls out a pendant on a long chain. He holds it out to me. A glittering blue gem in a golden setting dangles in the air between us.

"Wow, cool," I say.

After a moment, Mateo bunches the chain up and drops the necklace back into its pocket.

"Don't you need to wear that to do magic?" I ask.

"I won't be doing magic," Mateo says, eyes downcast.

"But you promised! You told me you'd teach me what you know."

"I told you I'd teach you about magic, not that I'd do any," he says. "Besides, I don't do magic anymore."

I wonder what happened to make Mateo swear off magic for

good, but I don't want to listen to some deep backstory. I want to learn.

"What are you going to teach me?"

"The most important thing you need to learn is how to control your powers."

"Okay," I say. "How can I do that?"

"Magic is tied to our emotions. When we can't control how we feel, we can't control our magic."

"But how would emotions affect magic?" There was nothing in the magic book about emotions, and Artemis hadn't said anything about that either. But I can't contradict Mateo without revealing the truth.

"Here's the way it was explained to me: magic is like one of our senses. So sometimes, if you get angry, you can't see straight, right? Your vision gets blurry. Magic is the same way but a lot more dramatic. Were you upset yesterday, in your backyard?"

"I wasn't upset. I was trying to conduct an experiment."

Mateo cocks an eyebrow at me. "And how did that go?"

"The experiment was unsuccessful," I admit.

"And how about in English class?"

"I might have been unprepared for the test, but I wasn't emotional about it."

Mateo stares at me, his face unreadable. "In poetry, when someone isn't very emotional, it's called being stoic. You seem stoic."

"I'm a scientist," I say. "I can't let emotion get in the way of facts."

"That's a good reason to learn self-control, then," Mateo says. "When I was first learning magic, I iced over my whole bedroom."

"Really?"

He smirks a little. "My parents found me throwing snowballs. I was seven. But the thing about ice is it melts. Everything was soaked. I had to throw out all my books. My parents were mad 'cause they had to replace the carpet. But I didn't mean to freeze everything. I just couldn't control my emotions."

"How did you learn to control them?"

"I have to think of something peaceful." He closes his eyes, a relaxed look coming over his face. "For me, it's a sunny beach. The waves come and go slowly. I think about the sound of the waves, count the seconds between them in my head."

I stare at Mateo. This sounds nothing like what the book said. He opens his eyes and sees me, and his cheeks turn a little red.

"You probably think it's stupid."

Yes.

"No, no," I say. "I'll, um, try it."

"Hold on." Mateo jumps up and dashes out of the room. When he comes back, he's holding a small cactus in a tiny clay pot. The cactus is only a couple inches tall. He sits back down and places the plant between us, right next to my stone.

"It's spiky, so please try not to stab us."

I square my shoulders and put my hands on my knees, then take a deep breath. I try not to think about my previous disastrous attempts at magic. If I want to be Artemis's apprentice, I need to get it under control, and I'm willing to try everything, even if I think it's silly.

I close my eyes. I picture a beach. I remember a few summers ago when my parents drove us down to Laguna Beach. I can hear the dogs barking along the boardwalk and the smell of sunscreen and salt saturating the air. That's the beach I imagine: the one with Catalina Island in the hazy distance and tourists splashing in the water. I remember standing waist-deep, too afraid to go deeper. A wave would slap against my chest and push me back a few feet, and then the water would rush toward the ocean, pulling me forward. I try to imagine the rhythmic pattern: the water pushes, the water pulls. Push, pull.

I hear Mateo let out a breath, but I don't open my eyes.

"You're doing great," he says.

His voice reminds me of Ingrid's that day, when a particularly strong wave knocked me down. Salt water burned my nose and eyes. She grabbed my arm and pulled me up, the sand chafing my skin where she held me.

"I'm not big enough," I said, sandy water spluttering out of my mouth.

"No," she said, "you're doing great."

The memories come flooding back: Ingrid and I climbing over the craggy rocks of the tide pools to search for hermit crabs. The two of us digging a giant hole until water began seeping through the bottom. The cold bite of the shower as we rinsed off the sand. Afterward, cramming into a booth with our parents in the tiny pizza shop by the boardwalk, realizing just how sunburned we were.

"Juniper." Mateo's voice, followed by a loud crack, breaks my concentration. "Juniper, stop, that's good."

I open my eyes. The cactus in front of me is four feet tall, at least, its lumpy arms leaning in wild, warped directions as it tips over sideways on the carpet. Mateo scoots quickly out of the way of its long spikes. The pot is in pieces, shattered by the engorged roots spilling onto the floor.

Mateo looks at me over the wreckage and gives me a hesitant smile. I can't help but beam back.

"Got a little wild at the end, but you did it," Mateo says, his smile growing into a grin. "You used magic."

Mateo and I spend the rest of the afternoon practicing. He hides the giant cactus in his closet and covers up the spilled dirt with a towel so that his tía won't notice. Then we practice on more than just plants. I manage to freeze a bottle of water, and it only explodes a little bit. Later, Tía Barbara brings us a plate of colorful conchas from the bakery down the street. I pick one with a spiral of pink sugar and bite into the sweet, fluffy bread. Mateo and I lean against the legs of his desk while we eat.

"Should we work on the English homework too?" Mateo asks between bites.

"I guess." I shove the rest of the concha in my mouth and wipe the pink dust on my jeans. I pull out the folder Mateo gave me and start skimming the assignment guidelines. "I hate poetry."

"You should give it a chance," Mateo says. "Poetry is a great way to just…feel."

I don't *want* to feel. But I don't say that.

"So we have to write our own poems," I say. "That should be a breeze for you."

"See? You're already using metaphors!" Mateo looks ecstatic, but I wrinkle my eyebrows together.

"I can barely understand poetry when I read it," I say. "How am I supposed to write it?"

"It's easy, really," he says. "You just think of something important to you. Or something you find weird or interesting. Me, I'm going to write about that weird house."

My eyes snap up to him. "What?"

"You know, that house next door to yours," he says. "It's the perfect subject for a poem, like you said. It's mysterious. Man, I wish I could go inside it."

Panic squeezes my chest. If Mateo finds out about the Elm House, he won't want to teach me magic anymore.

"You can't," I say quickly. "My mom says it's dangerous."

"My tía said that too," Mateo says, waving his hand dismissively. "But it's abandoned, right? What's the worst that could be in there? Mice?"

I swallow. I need to think of some reason for Mateo to stay away.

"Besides," he continues wistfully, "an old fence like that, I bet there's a rusted-out opening somewhere. Have you ever tried to get in?"

"No," I lie. "And you shouldn't go, trust me."

He shrugs.

"I'm still going to write about it. What will you write your poem about?"

I look down at the paper. After spending so much time with the magic book, regular words look so plain and ordinary. I don't want to write a poem. I want to observe the properties of magic and conduct experiments with Artemis. I don't care what Mateo says about magic leading to trouble. If magic is a science, like Artemis says, it can't be bad. Nothing bad can come from observing the properties of the universe. Like science, it's neutral. And I'd much rather be doing that than writing a stupid poem.

"I don't know," I say, rolling my eyes. "Butterflies, I guess?"

"Butterflies are poetic," Mateo says, nodding.

I open my notebook, but my mind is as blank as my paper. After a few minutes I look over at Mateo. He's already filled half his sheet with lines, crossing out words, filling them in, and doubling back. I don't understand how the words come so easily to him.

"This is hard," I grumble. "How do you even start?"

Mateo glances over to my paper, then back down at his own. He cocks his head to one side, thinking.

"Well, you picked butterflies," Mateo says. "Why? What do they mean to you? A poem isn't really about the thing that it's about. Usually, the subject represents something else. What do the butterflies represent?"

"They don't represent anything," I say. "They're just butterflies."

"But why do you like them so much?"

I think about all the hours I spent in the butterfly house at the university, letting the tiny legs of the lepidoptera land in my hair. I remember pedaling to remote areas of the nature preserve with Ingrid until I was out of breath and sore only to catch a split-second glimpse of the Blue. I think about the glass cases that line the walls of my house and my dad standing behind me with one hand on my shoulder, the other pointing out each butterfly as he sounded out its name.

"It kind of runs in the family," I say finally. "My dad's an entomologist, and my sister was too."

"I didn't know you had a sister."

"She died two years ago." I look down at the dark-blue carpet of Mateo's room. "I'm surprised you haven't heard about it."

"I'm sorry," he says. "I really didn't know."

I shrug. "It's okay. I don't talk about it a lot."

"Maybe you should," he says. "Or you could write poetry about it. Poetry can help you process your feelings. Like in this poem for class, the butterflies can represent family, and maybe the whole metamorphosis thing could represent the ways families change and—"

"I don't want to write about that," I say, and it comes out snappier than I meant it.

"Oh." Mateo blinks and leans back from me. I can tell he's hurt. "You don't have to. It's your poem. It was just an idea."

"I don't want to write a poem at all. And if I did, I wouldn't want butterflies to represent family," I say. "Families aren't supposed to change like butterflies. They're supposed to be there forever!"

I look up at Mateo, and he's staring at me, his pencil slipping from his fingers. Mateo's wrong. Poetry can't fix my problems. At least magic can do useful things, but poetry? Poetry won't bring Ingrid back.

Mateo starts to mumble something, but I'm not listening. A new idea spreads its wings in my mind. No, poetry can't bring Ingrid back.

But magic might.

I start to shove my things into my backpack.

"Are you okay?" Mateo asks.

"I have to go," I say, standing up and slinging my backpack over my shoulder. I'm halfway out the door when I turn around and lean back in. "Can I come back tomorrow? You'll teach me more magic?"

Mateo watches me from his spot on the carpet, looking bewildered. He nods, and that's all I need before I dash into the hallway.

"See you tomorrow!" I shout from the stairs. I run out the front door of Mateo's house and onto the sidewalk. Thick, gray clouds obscure the setting sun. The air smells like wet pavement. The wind rushes through my ears as I sprint the entire way back to my house.

I don't have time to think about poetry. Soren asked me what I hoped to gain from studying magic, and I figured it out. I'm going to gain something I never should have lost in the first place.

My sister.

It rains more during dinner. Not heavily, but enough that I can hear the beat of raindrops against the roof. I don't think it will be enough to explain the sudden growth spurt in our backyard, but I hope neither of my parents think to go back there anytime soon.

I can't talk about magic in front of my parents. When we marathoned the Harry Potter movies a few years ago, they couldn't stop pointing out the scientific impossibilities every chance they got. If that's how they reacted to fake magic, I could imagine how they'd react to real magic. It wouldn't be good.

Still, thoughts of magic rattle around in my head during dinnertime. My leg bounces up and down with the anticipation of running up to my room and reading more of the magic book. I want to go back over the notes Ruby made in that final chapter, "Of the Chaos." I need to know if my plan to bring Ingrid back will actually succeed.

"I have a question," I say through a mouthful of potatoes. "If you could somehow bring Ingrid back to life, would you?"

Mom looks down at her plate, and Dad chokes on a piece of chicken. Neither of them says anything at first. The only sound is Dad's coughing. Mom passes him a glass of water, and he takes a long drink. Far longer than necessary.

"We all miss Ingrid," Mom says finally.

"But if you woke up tomorrow, and she was back, like nothing happened. Wouldn't that be great?"

Dad's forehead wrinkles, and Mom glares at me.

"You know that's not possible, Juniper." Mom sounds more sad than angry. "We're not talking about impossible scenarios."

I shrink back in my chair. Ingrid died two years ago, but it feels like a lifetime ago.

"We never talk about Ingrid," I say. "It's like you want to forget her completely."

"Of course we don't want to forget about her." Dad sets his fork down with a clatter.

"Then why can't we talk about her?"

"We're not talking about this, Juniper," Mom says, dabbing her lips with a napkin. "We can talk about Ingrid if you want, but we're not talking about impossible scenarios."

I set my fork down. I'm not hungry anymore.

"You still didn't answer my question," I say.

Dad swirls the ice around his glass, his eyes fixed on the water, not on me.

"People can't come back from the dead, June." His voice is

quiet. Mom and Dad look at each other, sadness in their eyes. That's all the answer I need.

I mumble something about not thinking straight, and Mom gets out of her chair and walks around the table to give me a hug.

"I know you're having a hard time," she says. "Maybe we can do something fun this weekend to get your mind off things."

"I'm going over to Mateo's again tomorrow," I say.

Mom and Dad exchange a glance.

"I think that's a good idea," Mom says finally. "Mateo seems like a nice boy."

"His tía bought us conchas," I say.

"Conchas! Can I come hang out at Mateo's house too?" Mom laughs, and it's like the conversation about Ingrid never happened.

"I have more homework to catch up on," I say.

Soon we won't need to have sad conversations about Ingrid. Soon she'll sit at the table with us, eating dinner and laughing at Dad's jokes.

Upstairs, I sit down at my desk and pull out the heavy old book, along with my notebook. I open to the very last chapter, "Of the Chaos," and the image of the magician holding up his hands.

The power of life and death. It's something that I have. I don't have to just study it—I can put it to use. After all, what good is science if it's not useful?

This book has all the knowledge I need. The chemical composition of the human body. Diagrams of the circulatory and respiratory systems. There's a lot of mumbo jumbo about phlegm and bile and humors, but that's just medieval pseudoscience. Ruby's crossed things out and added her own notes, often replacing outdated names for elements with the modern ones. She's even put in her own ideas about the magical plane, how it can be used to invoke powerful magic like this.

I take thorough notes and make a list of materials. Maybe Artemis has some of these things already. I will talk to her about my plan tomorrow.

I know that this won't be easy. But now that I've decided, I can't stop mulling over the possibility in my mind. I climb into bed, but I can't make myself fall asleep. I lie there in the dark, fingers rubbing the stone in my palm as I stare at the ceiling. This is so much more than catching the world's rarest butterfly. I'm going to do something even more spectacular, even more impossible.

I'm going to bring Ingrid back to life.

Chapter 10

On Saturday, I wake up before the sun. It's too early to go to Artemis's house, although I wonder if she sleeps at all. So much has changed since I fell into the creek, but my old routine tugs at me. I slip on my socks and tiptoe carefully down the stairs.

In the dark, I navigate my way around the couch and over to the cases of butterflies hanging on the wall. Dad's replaced the glass and repinned all the specimens, but they're not perfect. There's another empty space in the case now: the Juniper Hairstreak I lost in my backyard. My eyes scan over to Dad's specimen of the Palos Verdes Blue. It's the smallest of the group, but even in this low light its wings shimmer. I look at it, but I don't dare touch the glass, not wanting to cause another accident.

Normally I spend my days poring over maps and calendars,

trying to figure out the best time and place to catch a Blue. But this past week, magic has consumed me. I feel guilty for having turned my back on entomology. I suddenly remember the science project that's due next week.

Back in my room, I pull out the rolled-up poster. The project should be simple—Chelsea said she would handle the diagrams and photos from the field trip, so I just need to do the written explanation. I unroll the poster board, and my breath catches in my throat.

When I think of a science project, I think of neatly drawn lines, of facts and figures—of clean, simple, and direct information. I think about the reports Dad pores over at night. They're all in uniform type and stacked neatly together.

This poster board is as far from that as I can imagine.

It doesn't look like a science project at all. It looks more like a collage in a scrapbook. At the top, in rainbow bubble letters, the title reads, "Plants and Animals of the Palos Verdes Nature Preserve." Beneath it, Chelsea has drawn cartoonish-looking animals: a fox with big anime eyes; an owl wearing a bow tie; flowers with faces. There are photos too, but none of them are of animals or plants. There's one of Chelsea and her two friends making peace signs in front of the ocean, another of Chelsea standing beside the tour guide, and then—most confusing of all—one of Chelsea and her friends' feet, mismatched socks in dirt-scuffed sneakers. Small doodles of flowers, trees, and butterflies clutter the margins, leaving barely enough room for me to add my written sections.

My hands shake as I look it over. I can't put my name on this. I can't turn this in as my project. What was Chelsea thinking? I start peeling off the photos and weird cartoonish diagrams. I run downstairs for my dad's book of local flora and fauna and get to work.

I trace some of the diagrams from the book onto my own paper and paste them on. I label everything properly, with scientific names and units on every measurement. When I'm done, everything is in straight rows, neat and orderly. Most of Chelsea's doodles are safely tucked beneath my own work. I paste the photos of her and her friends onto the bottom, as an end-note. I know she'll be upset if I get rid of them completely.

The sun is well into the sky by the time I finish, but the project actually looks like a science project now instead of something that belongs in art class. I roll the poster up and set it next to my backpack. The muffled sounds of my parents talking drift up from the kitchen, along with the smell of bacon. I make my way downstairs. Dad stands at the stove, and Mom sips coffee while she reads on her tablet.

"Sleep in today?" she asks.

I shrug and let her draw her own conclusions. When I sit down at the table, Dad slides a plate of bacon and eggs in front of me and pours me a cup of orange juice.

"When are you going to Mateo's house today?" Dad asks.

I want to go to Artemis's house first, but I can't tell them that.

"Probably after breakfast," I say. "I have a lot of homework to catch up on."

I've lied more in the past few days than I've ever lied in my life.

I shovel the eggs into my mouth as fast as I can, not wanting to waste any more daylight. Dad sits down next to me with his own plate.

"Have you seen the backyard lately?" he asks incredulously.

I choke on my eggs and have to take a gulp of orange juice before I can respond.

"Um, no?"

"The grass out there is insane," Dad says. "I have no idea how it got that long."

"I know how," Mom says. "*Someone* insists on cutting it themselves instead of hiring a gardener, but then neglects to actually do it."

"It's cheaper," Dad grumbles through a mouthful of bacon.

The conversation devolves into a discussion about how gardening services are a scam, so I excuse myself and go put on my last set of clothes that isn't stained with mud or grass. Once downstairs, I make sure my parents aren't looking through any of our windows before I slip out the front door and into the bushes.

I knock on the front door with the dragon-shaped knocker. No answer. Could they have gone out for the day? Just as I'm about to knock again, two large, yellow eyes appear in front of my face, and I jump back. Soren hangs upside down in front of me, gripping the eaves above the door with his feet. He blinks at me, swinging side to side.

"Back so soon?" he asks.

"You scared me!" I say, catching my breath.

He jumps down softly and sits upright, his striped tail wrapping around his body.

"Sorry about that," he says. "I was clearing a clog from one of the gutters."

"Is Artemis home?" I ask.

A loud thump and a curse from inside answer my question. Soren winces.

"You've gotten her quite worked up," Soren says, licking one of his hands. "I haven't seen her this excited about research in years. She's been doing a bit of spring cleaning."

The door flies open, and Artemis appears holding a large cardboard box. Her hair, normally stacked neatly on top of her head, is spilling around her shoulders. Her sleeves are rolled up, and her shirt is half-untucked from her skirt.

"All this rubbish is in the way!" Artemis shouts. She hurls the box onto the patio, an enormous dust cloud erupting in its wake. I take a step back, coughing, trying not to get any dust in my eyes. Artemis wipes her hands on her skirt, but it was already so dusty I'm not sure it did much good.

"Ah, Juniper! Just the girl I wanted to see." She grabs my wrist and pulls me into the house, and I have to be careful not to trip over Soren.

All the doors and windows in the house have been thrown

open. I peer through the door to the library to see stacks of books pulled off the shelves. I can't look for long—Artemis drags me up the stairs, following a trail of loose papers to her study.

Artemis's study looks completely upended. Papers, inkpots, and jars of herbs lay scattered around the floor. Books slump over on the shelves, and more are stacked on every possible surface. Much of the clutter I saw last time has been swept aside, into boxes or heaped into sacks on the floor. The beams of the light from the window illuminate the dust drifting through the room, disturbed from its long rest.

"I've been clearing space," Artemis says breathlessly as I stare at the chaos. "Pulling out all my old research on the magical plane."

She gestures to the wall behind me. I turn and see maps, diagrams, and charts pinned up, Artemis' looping handwriting scrawled over all of them. I recognize a map of the nature preserve and another of the entirety of Southern California, both dotted with pins.

"You're going to need to do a bit more light reading," Artemis says from behind me. I turn back around and see her holding a stack of books towering higher than her head.

"Um."

She places the stack down on a stool and turns toward the desk, her hands rummaging around the papers.

"I'll have to get you caught up on the equipment and the terms and what we've learned so far—oh! I'll need to pick up some supplies, but I'll have to go to Santa Monica for those…"

Artemis talks so fast I can't follow. I look at the stack of books, apprehension like a rock in my gut. I don't want to have to do that much reading before we start experimenting. I want to ask Artemis about my idea, but she's so absorbed in her own thoughts I can't get a word in.

Soren slinks into the room. I look at him, and I wonder if he can sense how nervous I am.

"Let's calm down a bit, shall we?" He jumps up onto the desk so that he's tall enough to place a small hand on Artemis's shoulder. "Might I suggest tea?"

I'm glad Soren is here, a calm voice amongst the chaos. Even Artemis pauses and takes a deep breath before clapping her hands together.

"Splendid idea, Soren," she says. "Clear a spot for the tray, will you, Juniper?"

Artemis leaves the room in as much of a whirlwind as she entered. I look around. There aren't many places to sit, now that there are notes and books and scraps of paper everywhere, but I manage to clear a small space on the couch. The desk is a lost cause for the tray, but I remove a stack of books from a short stool and drag it over.

"She's been up all night," Soren tells me, perching on the back of the sofa.

"I didn't mean to cause so much…" I gesture around the room at the general chaos, unsure of what to call it.

"Artemis and I have been studying magic for a long time," he says. "I'm used to her moods."

"How long has it been, exactly?" I ask.

"Time is different for me now." Soren blinks. "I couldn't say how many years. But there were no airplanes like the ones that cut across the sky today. We came to America on a large ship."

"A ship!" How long have airplanes been around? At least a hundred years. "But how?"

"Well it sits on the water, see—"

"No, I mean, how is it possible that you and Artemis have studied magic so long? You don't seem very old."

"Magic changes things," Soren says, his voice low and grave. "It lives by its own rules. It exerts its own control over life. And death."

I shiver at his words. *Life and death*. If magic could make Artemis and Soren live over a hundred years, maybe it really could help me bring Ingrid back to life.

"Artemis has forgotten the past," he says. "I am afraid she's destined to repeat it."

"Repeat what?"

Soren scratches his head with his claws, as if he's trying to remember.

"These experiments, about the magical plane. She's conducted them before, you know."

"And were they successful?" I ask hopefully.

"They may have been her greatest failure," Soren says. "And they are dangerous. Very dangerous. Her previous apprentice,

Ruby, was lost."

Lost. Artemis said she lost her apprentice, but she never said how. Was there some sort of accident? I want to ask, but I hear Artemis's footsteps on the stairs.

"Maybe things will be different this time," I say. I have to believe in Artemis. She might be odd, but she's the only person that takes my quest for scientific knowledge seriously. And she's my only hope for getting Ingrid back.

Soren hops off the couch and slinks back toward the door.

"I hope, for your sake, that they are."

He doesn't look at me as he slips out of the room.

Artemis returns with a teapot and two teacups on a tray. She shoves aside a stack of papers and sets the tray down on the desk. She yawns, looking much calmer than she had when I first arrived. I watch her pour two cups, wondering how she'll react when I tell her my plan.

She hands me my teacup and sits on the arm of the couch. I take a sip—the tea is strong and bitter, which I usually despise, but there's also something floral and sweet about it that leaves me wanting more.

Artemis takes a sip of her own tea and sighs, looking around the room. I have to say something now, before she gets distracted again.

"Can I ask you something?"

"Inquiry is the heart of science," she says. "Go on."

"I..." I look into my teacup, choking on the words. "Do you think it's possible for magic to bring somebody back to life?"

Artemis takes a long sip of tea, peering at me over her teacup.

"Resurrection," she says finally. "Or necromancy, as some call it."

I wince. Out loud, it sounds silly. Of course it's not possible—there's no scientific basis for bringing someone back to life. I feel foolish for getting my hopes up.

"I know it sounds ridiculous—"

"Oh, no," Artemis interrupts. "Not ridiculous at all. With the power of science, anything is possible. But it is very difficult. You are talking about using your powers not just on plants and insects, but on larger life-forms. On humans."

I tremble with excitement as Artemis speaks. She doesn't dismiss the idea as impossible or ridiculous, like my parents did. She actually listens to me. I unzip my backpack and pull out *Alchymy, Magicks, and Natural Philosophy*. I flip to the final chapter: "Of the Chaos."

"I've been comparing the text to Ruby's annotations," I say, holding up the book. "The text says we need these ingredients. Ruby's notes outline the exact conditions necessary for the magical plane to imbue the magician with enough power to make it work. I think that with the right materials, under the right conditions, we can do it."

Artemis leans closer, her eyes scanning the pages. She takes a another long, agonizingly slow sip of tea.

"Since we're going to be researching the magical plane anyway," I continue, "I thought we could do this experiment too."

Artemis tips her head and stares into my eyes. I try to stare back with just as much fierce determination, hoping that her response is not as negative as my parents'.

"I'm impressed by your tenacity," she says finally. I don't know what *tenacity* means, but my heart swells anyway—I want to impress her. "Tell me, who is it that you want to bring back so badly?"

"Ingrid. My sister."

"Ah." Artemis sets her teacup down. When she speaks, her voice is gentle. "Tell me about her. What inspires you to bring her back?"

"Ingrid was...everything I want to be." My hand shakes, so I grip my teacup tighter. "She was the smartest person I knew. Smarter than my dad, even. They'd always have these heated conversations about entomology. I didn't know very much about it at the time, but I wanted to be just like her. I even cut my hair like hers after she...left. Short hair like a scientist. Dad called her 'pragmatic,' because everything she did was so exact and calculated."

My voice catches, and I set the teacup down. The night she died must have been a serious miscalculation.

"The scientific mind certainly runs in your family," Artemis says. "But what was she like as a sister?"

"As a sister?" I wrinkle my forehead. I don't see the difference—Ingrid was Ingrid. Science was her whole life, and now it's mine.

"You know," Artemis says. "The secret language, the heated arguments. The sisterly bonds."

Sisterly bonds. The first time Ingrid took me with her to the nature preserve, I struggled to keep up with her. I tripped and scraped my knee so bad it bled. I remember the burning feeling of keeping my tears inside, not wanting my cool, calm sister to see me be so weak. I thought she'd leave me behind. But she didn't. She came back for me, cleaned my knee, bandaged it without flinching, and then hugged me. I remember this hug in particular because I'd wanted so badly to impress her. I was mad at myself for falling and getting hurt before I'd even gotten the chance. But then it didn't matter, because she wrapped her arms around me and held my hand the whole way home.

I forgot about that. When I remember Ingrid, I remember her as a strong, confident scientist with a bright future. I don't think about the moments where she held my hand or leaned on my shoulder. For two years, I remembered her love in the moments she let me be a part of her work. Collecting butterflies. Finding the Palos Verdes Blue. It was our secret language. I could continue those, even without her.

But all the other things that I can't do without her? I don't think about those. I don't think about the time we snuck extra

Christmas cookies from the kitchen and hid them under our beds, only to wake up in the morning to an ant invasion. I don't think about how, when I was too scared to climb down from the jungle gym at the park, she sat underneath me for hours trying to calm me down until Dad found us. I don't think about the time we fought over the TV remote and ended up flinging it into the screen, leaving a permanent dead spot in the display.

My eyes burn, but I don't let myself cry. I grip my knees with my palms, fingernails digging hard into my skin. A good scientist doesn't let emotion get in the way of their work. I've tried not to think about Ingrid emotionally. It's easy to think of Ingrid as a scientist because that is something I can be on my own. But it's harder to think of Ingrid as a sibling, because I can't be a sister without her.

"A world without Ingrid is like a world without magic," I say, fighting to keep my voice even. I don't look away from Artemis's eyes. "How can I live in a world like that when I know there's a way I can fix everything?"

The corner of Artemis's lip quirks upward. She puts a firm hand on my shoulder.

"You are strong, Juniper," she says. "Stronger than you know."

I keep my hands on my knees, waiting. Finally, she lets out a small sigh.

"Strong *and* determined." She stands up and goes to the window. "While I have attempted similar experiments, I have never tried something of this magnitude. But I've never held the intense power that you naturally hold, either. With my experience, and your magic, it might be possible."

"Really?"

"But it will be risky," she says, glancing over her shoulder at me. "And the timing of it will be of the utmost importance. The magical plane is a fickle thing—it comes in phases like the moon. But if we time it right, we might be able to harness enough energy to make it work."

I jump up, bumping into the tray of teacups. Tea sloshes onto the floor.

"You really mean it?" I ask. "You will help me?"

"I will help you," Artemis says. "But I do ask for something in exchange."

"Anything," I say. Anything is worth Ingrid's life.

"Once it's done, you will help me with an experiment that I have long attempted but has never been successful."

"What's the experiment?"

"It involves the magical plane," Artemis says. "I believe it is possible to go there and return. I request your assistance in testing this theory."

"Yes," I say quickly. "I want to help. I want to be your assistant."

"Excellent." The look in her eyes is like the one Dad gets whenever he looks at an interesting insect—excitement.

Artemis crosses the room to a file cabinet and pulls open the bottom drawer with an explosion of dust.

"No…not that one…no," she murmurs as she digs through

the contents. "Aha!"

She pulls out a dusty notebook with a faded cover and flips through the pages.

"Here are the elements we need. I have most of them in my storeroom, and I can acquire the rest easily. I'll need to adjust the ratios to correct for Ingrid's size...but overall, these measurements should be similar."

I scan the list of elements: carbon, ammonia, water, phosphorus, iron, and a bunch of other things I don't recognize the names of.

"These are just the materials. What about the process?"

Artemis shuts the notebook and smiles.

"The process is the tricky part. Half of magic is the wanting—I'm sure you've discovered that as you've experimented. I believe that with your passion and powers, and my calculations for the perfect conditions, it will work."

"That doesn't sound very scientific."

Artemis shrugs.

"We won't know until we try, will we? I have my hypothesis, now all we need to do is the experiment. That's the very foundation of science, is it not?"

She's right. We have to try it. But I can't crush the nervous feeling in my stomach. Artemis must be able see it, because she purses her lips.

"Would you like to try it on something smaller, first? A beloved deceased pet, perhaps?"

"No," I say. "No, I can do it."

"There's one more material I'll need, but it's not something I can get," she says, consulting the notebook again. "One missing element. I need you to bring a small artifact—something important to Ingrid. A necklace, perhaps, or some other keepsake. Something she cherished. Can you do that?"

I nod. "I'll find something."

"Good, good." She sets the notebook down. "I will need to consult my charts, but I believe the ideal time will be soon. If we miss our window, we may have to wait several months."

"How soon?" I ask.

"A matter of days," Artemis says. "Be ready. I will fetch you when it's time. Bring your stone and your artifact. I'll bring everything else."

My head swirls. After two years of missing Ingrid, I can't believe this will happen so soon. I don't think about what artifact I will choose or how I will explain to my parents why Ingrid will suddenly be back from the dead. All I think about is coming home from school and seeing her shoes by the front door.

"I'll be ready," I say.

"Well then, Juniper Edwards," Artemis says, a grin spreading across her face. "Let's bring a human back to life."

Chapter 11

It's early afternoon by the time I make it to Mateo's house. I bounce on my toes as I wait for him to answer the door. I can't shake the exciting feeling I got at the Elm House.

The door swings open, and Tía Barbara stands in the doorway. Her curly hair is pulled back. The lines in her face deepen as she smiles.

"Ah, Juniper! Just in time for lunch."

I step inside, and a strong scent of spices hits my nose. I look around, but I don't see Mateo.

"I sent Mateo to get some milk," she says, shutting the door. "He'll be back any minute. Come, you can get started."

I follow her to the kitchen. A pot sizzles on the stove. Tía Barbara opens a cupboard and pulls out a package of corn tortillas.

"Do you like menudo?" she asks.

"Um," I say. "I don't think I've had it before."

She beckons me over to the stove and pulls the lid off the pot. Inside is a brothy, orange soup. I see pieces of beef, and there's huge chunks of zucchini and corn and a light green vegetable that almost looks like a pear. There's also a bunch of plump, round beans.

"It's soup," she says. "There are onions and cilantro for the top, and I've got tortillas."

She turns the knob on the stove and the gas clicks to life. She places a tortilla right on top of the burner, the flame licking at the bottom. I worry it will catch on fire, but after a few moments she flips it over. The side that touched the flame has some dark brown spots but isn't burned. She does this again and again, stacking the tortillas on a plate.

"Would you like to put it in the bowls?" she asks, handing me a ladle.

"I can do that."

I take the ladle and start scooping the soup into bowls, trying to balance how many vegetables I put in. I'm not used to soup with the vegetables in big chunks. Tía Barbara continues heating the tortillas while I scoop beside her.

"Tía! I'm back!"

Mateo appears in the kitchen archway. He's got a bicycle helmet in one hand and a gallon of milk in the other. His hair is squished down, some of it stuck to his forehead with sweat.

"Oh, hey, Juniper," he says when he sees me. "My aunt gave you a job already."

"I wanted to be helpful," I say, waving the ladle.

"You were very helpful," Tía Barbara says. "Now go sit down, both of you—it's time to eat."

Mateo and I sit at the oval dining room table. It's big enough to seat ten people, but half is cluttered with framed photographs of Mateo's family. There are pictures of weddings and graduations and baptisms interspersed with Christmas cards in both English and Spanish. My eyes scan the anonymous faces until they land on one in particular: There's a man with short black hair standing beside a smiling woman with curly, bleached-blond hair. Between them is a little boy with a huge mass of curls on his head, smiling a gap-toothed smile.

"Is that you?" I ask, pointing at the photo.

"Maybe," Mateo says, but the way he turns red tells me that it is.

"Are those your parents? The ones still in Seattle?"

"Yeah." Mateo looks away.

We're quiet as Tía Barbara puts two steaming bowls of menudo in front of us. She goes back into the kitchen to grab the onions and cilantro.

"I'm sorry," I say quietly.

"It's okay," he says. Then, "I miss them."

I don't know what to say. I poke at a large chunk of zucchini with my spoon, and it's so soft it easily splits into two. I want to ask Mateo more about what happened in Seattle, but Tía Barbara comes to the table with the plate of tortillas and a bowl of limes, and it's too late.

"Try it," she urges.

I lift a spoonful to my mouth. The soup is delicious—all of the flavors blend together in a soft and savory way. I add onions and cilantro and squeeze limes onto the top, just like Mateo does. I scoop some of the meat and the vegetables into the tortilla and eat it like a sloppy, wet taco, which makes Mateo laugh. When we're done eating, Mateo and I help Tía Barbara with the dishes.

"I'll put some in a container to bring home for your parents," she says.

"Thanks." I know my parents will be happy if I bring home the soup, if only because it proves to them that I am capable of making friends.

I'm still not sure if Mateo is really a friend. I guess if you go over to a person's house and eat lunch with them, and you don't hate the experience, they might be a friend. But Mateo likes poetry, and I like science. Mateo thinks magic is bad and shouldn't be done, and I think magic is amazing and worthy of study. We're too different to be friends, just like me and Chelsea. I put the limes into a small plastic bag and think about how this isn't a friendship. It's more like a scientific research relationship. That describes it a lot better.

Once the food is portioned out and put away, Mateo and I go up to his room. He closes the door and walks to the middle of the room and sits cross-legged, like he did yesterday.

"I had an idea while I was riding home from the store," he says. He reaches into his pockets and pulls out fistfuls of leaves and twigs and sets them on the floor in front of him. I sit on the other side of the pile.

"And the idea is…?"

"Well, we've tried your magic with things that are still alive," he says. "But these things are all dead!"

I think about the pencil and paper in English class and the paper towels in the girls' bathroom.

"It should still work, based on previous observations," I say.

"Maybe if you practice doing it on purpose, it'll be less random," he says. "You can get a feel for the magic and know when it's about to happen."

Mateo and I spend the afternoon turning dry brown leaves into bright green ones. Some of the leaves even grow, going from the size of my thumb to the size of a dinner plate. But even more amazing is a stick. I hold it like a pencil, and it gradually turns green. A yellow rose emerges from one end. I flinch as thorns prick my skin. Mateo puts the rose in a glass of water.

After a few hours I look around the room, now carpeted with broad green leaves.

"I don't understand why you think magic is bad," I say.

"Maybe it's not all bad," he says.

Mateo picks up a leaf and twists it in his fingers.

"Last year, there was an accident," he says, not meeting my

eyes. "I…hurt someone. With magic."

The leaf cracks in his hands, and he drops it.

"I didn't mean to," he says. "Well…I kind of did. There was this kid who was just a real jerk, you know? And he pushed a girl into the grass while the sprinklers were on. She got really upset and cried. So I pushed him into the sprinklers back."

"That doesn't sound like it would hurt," I say.

"No, but the ice did," Mateo says. "I froze the water. I was so mad that I wanted it to hurt. He'd hurt so many people, and I wanted him to feel the pain too. I realized that day just how sharp ice shards can be."

I think about ice sharp enough to cut through strangling vines. "Did he…die?"

"No! But I was upset, and I lost control. His clothes and his skin got all cut up. There was a lot of blood."

I shiver, thinking about the plants that nearly strangled me.

"There was no proof that I did it, obviously, because no one there knew about magic," he says. "But I knew. And my parents knew. And even if that guy doesn't understand how I did it, he knows it was me."

"So that's why your parents sent you to live with your aunt?" I ask.

Mateo nods.

"My parents are both magicians," he says. "They're the ones who taught me. And so is Tía Barbara."

"Your *aunt* is a magician?" I ask. "Just how many magicians are there?"

"Shh!" he says, glancing nervously at his bedroom door. "We can't tell her. I'm strictly forbidden from using magic. And if she knows that you have magic, she might not let us hang out."

"I can keep a secret," I say. "Are there any more magicians in the neighborhood I should know about?"

"I don't know any," Mateo says. "In Seattle, my parents had a lot of magic friends. It mostly gets passed down through families, taught in secret, but magicians tend to find each other."

Mateo smiles. He picks up the broken leaf he dropped and runs his fingers over it. The leaf stitches itself back together, whole again.

"You know, I think I'm changing my mind."

"About what?" I ask.

"After the accident, I thought magic could only lead to bad things," he says. "But now that I've seen you doing it, I'm starting to think it can also be used for good."

I look at the leaf in Mateo's hands. He's taught me a lot about magic. He likes to hang out with me, even if I don't like poetry. His aunt made me soup. For some reason, I feel like I can trust Mateo. Maybe if I tell him about my plan, he'll understand. After all, what better use for magic than to reunite a family?

"There's something I want to do," I say quietly.

"Oh yeah? Something else you want to try?"

"No." I shake my head. "I have a plan. To use magic for good."

"What is it?"

131

"Well, if I can bring leaves and butterflies to life, why not something bigger?"

"Like an animal?"

"Like a person."

Mateo leans back. "Whoa. You're not serious?"

"I am serious," I counter. "My sister died two years ago, and with magic, maybe I can bring her back."

Mateo shakes his head, his brown eyes wide.

"No, Juniper, you can't," he says. "People can't come back from the dead."

My throat tightens. This isn't going how I planned.

"That's what my dad said."

"Your dad's right."

"No!" I shout. I shouldn't have told him. I thought he would understand. I thought he would think it was good. But I was wrong. "He's not. It can be done."

"How do you know? You just got magic two weeks ago. Trust me, that kind of magic is bad news. Messing with life and death. It's unnatural."

"Lots of people think science is unnatural," I say. "Modern medicine is unnatural, but you don't refuse to get X-rays, do you?"

"Well, no—"

"Besides, I've been doing my own research in addition to our experiments," I say. "There's no reason why it shouldn't work."

"What do you mean, your own research?"

I pull my backpack over and pull out *Alchymy, Magicks, and*

Natural Philosophy. I drop it with a heavy thunk between us, then turn to the final chapter, "Of the Chaos." I turn it around to face Mateo.

"See? It's all there," I say. "The ingredients, the process. I have to try."

Mateo stares at the book.

"Juniper, this book is like a million years old."

"Nearly four hundred," I correct.

"Still, you can't trust this! Where did you even get this?"

"I found it. At the library."

Mateo stares at me like I'm an insect that grew an extra thorax.

"At the library," he repeats. "Juniper, you can't seriously consider doing this."

"I'm not just considering it," I say. "I'm doing it. You said yourself magic can be used for good. This will be good. Having Ingrid back will be good."

Mateo slowly shakes his head.

"Magic can't fix everything, Juniper," he says. "You have to accept that."

The rose in the glass quivers. The carpet of leaves twitches and shakes. Mateo scrambles backward. I'm not doing it on purpose, but my hands are shaking with anger, and so are the leaves. Slowly, they begin to rise into the air.

"Juniper," he says warily. "Pull it back, Juniper."

"What good is learning to control my magic if I don't use it for anything?" I shout.

I can't see Mateo's face. Dozens and dozens of leaves hang in the air between us. This is why a scientist needs to be selective about who they choose to share their research with. Dad is always telling me about his colleagues that don't believe in his projects. I repeat what he says to me every time someone gets him down.

"You're going to eat your words," I say.

With a loud crunch, each leaf simultaneously shrivels back into its brown, dead form. The leaves fall apart, sprinkling across Mateo's room like confetti. I slam the book shut and slide it back into my backpack. How could I have been stupid enough to trust Mateo? I knew he wasn't a real friend. We are too different. He doesn't understand. I walk to the door.

"When I have my sister back, I won't need you. I won't need anyone. Magic can fix it. You'll see."

I don't look back as I run down the stairs. I'm almost to the front door when Tía Barbara calls to me. She's sitting in a recliner reading a magazine.

"Ah, don't forget the menudo!" She jumps up, runs to the kitchen and retrieves a container tied in a plastic bag. "You're in a hurry."

"Sorry," I mumble. "Thanks."

I hear Mateo's footsteps on the stairs, and I dash out of the house before he can catch up with me.

When I get home, I don't want to talk to Mom and Dad about how things went at Mateo's house. I don't want to see the look of disappointment on their faces when they realize my only lead on friendship didn't work out. I don't want them to ask me what happened or make suggestions about how I can fix things, like they always do. I want to focus on what really matters: bringing Ingrid back to life.

I put the menudo in the fridge and run upstairs before my parents can intercept me. Dad's in the garage, and Mom's watching TV in the living room, so by the time they realize I'm home, I'm already in my room.

I spend the evening poring over the book. I try to take my own notes, but every time I do, moss starts growing over the page, obscuring my words. After the fifth ruined page of notebook paper, I give up. Instead I read Ruby's scrawled annotations over and over until I've committed them to memory.

Carbon, ammonia, water, phosphorus, iron. The magical plane. The strength of the magician's will. These are all things I have or Artemis will supply. When it comes to will, I definitely have enough of it. I want Ingrid back more than anything in the world, and I'm willing to do whatever it takes to make it happen.

Mom knocks on my door to let me know dinner is ready, and I look up from the book, bleary-eyed, surprised to see that it's already dark. The only light in my room is the desk lamp.

"I'm not hungry," I say, positioning myself so that she can't see the book on my desk.

"I'll put a plate in the microwave for you," she says.

When she's gone, I turn back to the book. I pull the stone out of my pocket and place it on my desk. The wavering glow reminds me of what Mateo taught me—the waves of the ocean hitting a beach. I try to push Mateo out of my mind. For this, I won't need to hold back.

I tear off bits of the ruined notebook paper as I read, rolling them into tiny balls, like little seeds. I close them in my hand, then open it, revealing small, yellow flowers. My own small magic trick. I drop them into a pile on the desk, and by the time I'm finished reading "Of the Chaos" for the third time, I have a small mountain of yellow flowers.

A quiet, familiar tap, tap, tap catches my attention.

Outside the window, Soren sits perched on the roof tiles. I slide the window open, and he hops in, carefully sidestepping the pile of flowers. He dips a hand into them and lets the little yellow flowers trickle between his fingers.

"Impressive work," he says.

"I needed something to do with my hands," I say. "What are you doing here?"

"I came to deliver a message," he says. "Artemis has consulted her instruments, and there is a short window of time tomorrow night that is ideal for the experiment."

"*Tomorrow?*"

It's been two years without Ingrid—two years without hiding under blankets during thunderstorms, two years without quizzing each other on the scientific names of native species to see who could remember the most (it was always her). My chest feels like it's going to explode at the idea that tomorrow, I'll be able to do all those things with her again. Tomorrow, everything will be perfect.

"Are you having doubts?" Soren asks.

"No," I say. "I just didn't expect it to be so soon. Is Artemis... preparing?"

"She popped over to Santa Monica for some supplies," he says. "Poor timing, unfortunately, as Saturday nights in Santa Monica are teeming with unsavory sorts."

"Is Artemis considered an 'unsavory sort'?" I ask.

"By some," Soren says, amused.

"Well, thank you for the message. I have some of my own preparations to make."

I turn back to the book, but Soren remains still.

"There is another reason for my visit," he says. "I want to warn you."

"If you're going to try to convince me not to go through with it, don't bother."

Soren's tail flicks like an annoyed cat.

"You have the same stubborn tenacity that gets Artemis into trouble," he says. "It makes her a great magician, true, but there is no shortage of trouble that comes along with it."

"I don't care if there's trouble, Soren," I tell him. "I have to get my sister back."

"There's no guarantee it will work."

"But I have to try. If I don't, I will always wonder what things would be like if I had."

"A wise sentiment," Soren agrees. "But applied naively. This experiment you are undertaking is dangerous, but you should be wary of Artemis herself."

"Artemis? Why?"

"As I said, Artemis is a brilliant magician and an amazing scientist," he says. "But she has a tendency to disregard the feelings and well-being of others in the pursuit of knowledge. I do not consider her bad a person. After all, we have been companions for…well, a very long time. But over the years, people have gotten hurt because she pushed them too far or got so caught up in whatever she was attempting that she was willing to risk their lives."

"Scientists have to take risks," I say. "Like Marie Curie. She contributed a lot to science, even though she got radiation poisoning in the process."

Soren sighs and puts a small hand over his face.

"I have seen so many like you but none as young as you," he says. "You are a child, Juniper, though a powerful one. I fear that Artemis will try to use you for her own devices."

"I don't care if she uses me, as long as I get my sister back," I tell him. "It's worth the risk. And besides, if you think she's so bad, why do you hang around her and deliver her messages? You're the one who told me to visit her in the first place."

"She'd been better recently," he says. "We'd been living a quiet life, gardening, reading, reminiscing...and when we noticed you, I thought it might be nice to have a visitor. I did not expect your presence to ignite such a fervor in her. I am not blaming you, of course—it's just that you are so very similar. In your eyes I can see the same burning passion I saw in hers all those years ago, when we were both young apprentice magicians in London trying to make our way in the world."

I use my finger to draw absentminded spirals in my pile of flowers.

"You've done this for a long time, Soren, but I'm just getting started. I have to try."

Soren sighs.

"I had to try, as well," he says. He hops back into the windowsill. "Good night, Juniper. Be ready. And be careful."

PART IV
Experiment

Chapter 12

I slip out of my bedroom at midnight. Ingrid's room is beside mine and hasn't been used since she died. A sign hangs on her door that says INGRID LANE with a silhouette of a dolphin. She got it on a family trip to Sea World. Mom keeps the door handle dusted, so it looks just as clean as any of the other door handles, shiny and golden, as if we go in all the time. But the truth is that the room is the same as it was two years ago.

When I push open the door, the air smells stale. The air doesn't smell like Ingrid anymore. Ingrid smelled like moist earth and salt air. Like home. I can remember it clearly, but the smell is long gone.

Ingrid was two years older than me, and it's been two years since she died. It hits me that I'm her age now. That the room I'm in belonged to a girl just like me, in the seventh grade, figuring out where to sit at lunch and how to make friends. I wonder if Ingrid hated poetry. A thrill runs through me when I realize that tomorrow night, I'll be able to ask her.

Ingrid always kept her bed made and her room tidy. Her desk is exactly as she left it—pens lined up in a row beside a notebook, papers stacked tidily in the corner. Mom and Dad come in to vacuum the floor and dust the shelves every once in a while, since Ingrid hated dust. Everything had to be clean.

Her walls are papered with drawings. I'd forgotten that Ingrid liked to draw. She didn't consider herself an artist, even though she was very good at it. "I'm just drawing what I see," she'd say. The pictures on the walls are all of things in nature, bugs and strange flowers and interesting plants. They're as anatomically correct and perfectly proportioned as can be. But what really stand out are her butterflies.

I consider myself a decent nature sketcher, but Ingrid's butterflies are beautiful and vivid and flawless. She's captured the delicate fuzz of the abdomen and the gentle curve of the proboscis, the long, tubular mouth. Almost all of them are of her favorite lepidoptera—the Palos Verdes Blue. She has dozens of drawings, all from different angles. I remember now the hours she spent drawing, frustrated that she could never get it just right.

The Blue was Ingrid's favorite butterfly, and blue was her favorite color. Her bed is blue, her chair is blue. She wanted to paint her walls blue, but Mom said no. Whenever we went to the hardware store, we'd look at paint chips together. Ingrid skipped past colors like "robin's egg" and "summer sky." None of them were perfect. None of them were Palos Verdes Blue.

There's a jewelry box on her dresser, but I won't find something meaningful there. Ingrid didn't like wearing jewelry. I consider taking down one of the pictures of the butterflies, but that doesn't seem right either. She drew so many of them, I remember, because none of them were perfect. Each was slightly different, but each still *wrong* to her. I remember what she said to me each time we saw the Palos Verdes Blue in our dad's butterfly collection, the one he got from the butterfly house at the university.

"It's not the same," she would say. "It's not *real*."

I wish that we'd caught one together before she died. That would be something special to her—a real, wild Palos Verdes Blue. But we didn't. In the two years since she's been gone, I haven't been able to get one either.

I'll have to bring the second-best thing.

I leave everything as it was and step back into the hall, closing the door behind me. Next time I go into her bedroom, Ingrid will be going in with me.

Downstairs, in the dark, I carefully remove the Palos Verdes Blue from Dad's butterfly case, hoping he won't notice. Thankfully, none of the butterflies come to life this time.

I don't want to damage the wings, so I slip it carefully into an empty, washed-out tin that used to hold mints. I slip the tin into my sweatshirt pocket. Of all the things in the universe, what better represents Ingrid than the one thing she wanted most?

I can't sleep that night. I'm too busy thinking about Ingrid and what things will be like once she's back. I wonder if she's ever tried menudo.

The next morning, Dad wakes me up just before noon and tells me I've been sufficiently well-behaved the past few days that it's time I'm set loose. I'm allowed to ride my bike today, with a few conditions: I have to be home by dinnertime, and I can't go anywhere near the nature preserve.

When I set off down the road on my bike, I don't have a plan. My go-to spot is usually the nature preserve, but even if it wasn't off limits, they do guided hikes on Sundays, and I like to avoid people. I end up riding the other way, past the school and toward the main road. There are blocks and blocks of strip malls, but I don't have any money. I go past the strip malls and into the hills, where the houses get bigger and there are fewer cars. I round a corner, and a church with a tall, white steeple comes into view. The parking lot is packed with the Sunday crowd. My family doesn't go to church, but I stop on the sidewalk.

Beside the church is the graveyard. Ingrid is buried there.

I didn't mean to come here on purpose, but now that I'm here, I have an urge to go in. In the two years since she's died,

I've never visited her grave, not since she was buried. Mom and Dad have come, but I've always stayed home. There's no logical reason to visit a grave. I've always found it more uncomfortable than comforting. Besides, after tonight, it won't matter, because Ingrid will be back.

And yet I find myself leaning my bike up against the metal fence and walking inside. There's a large group of people dressed in black, so I avoid the main path and take the long way around. I know exactly where Ingrid's grave is. The memory of burying her is burned into my mind. I can smell the same scent of u pended earth. The sky that day was clear, cloudless blue. It felt so wrong for the weather to be so perfect, for people to continue on with their lives as if nothing had changed. The world didn't notice Ingrid was gone, but *I* lost my whole world.

I stop in front of her grave. It looks different now. What was a mound of dirt is now completely grown over with grass. Her tombstone, black marble with white words engraved onto the surface, is water-spotted from the recent rain.

My eyes prickle. At my feet, white flowers start to blossom in the grass, and I let them. So close to Ingrid, it feels like these flowers are for her.

"I'm sorry," I say, unsure why. I know Ingrid isn't really there. But I can't stop. "I haven't caught the Blue yet. I've been trying."

A gentle breeze brushes against my cheek. I feel the spindly stems of the flowers brush against my ankles. They aren't strangling me as they did before. Instead they're gentle, as if they're trying to comfort me.

"Maybe I wasn't meant to catch it yet. Maybe I can't do it unless you're with me."

I sit down and lean against the headstone. The grass rustles and tickles my skin. Ingrid is so close, but so far. I feel the tendrils of plants snaking their way around my feet and hands. I close my eyes and think about how different the world will be tonight, when Ingrid is beside me and not beneath me.

A shadow passes over me, and I jolt awake. A tall figure stands in front of me. I didn't realize I'd fallen asleep. The sun is sinking low behind the hills, and it's almost getting dark. The parking lot beyond the fence is empty, the funeral procession gone.

"I've been looking for you."

Artemis stands in front of me, wearing a dark wool cloak with a moon-shaped clasp. The hood is down, revealing her hair tied in a low bun at the nape of her neck. She looks otherworldly.

I lift my hand to wipe my eyes and feel the thin stems of the flowers snap. They've climbed all over me, encasing my legs in a fine web of green. I pull myself up, brushing the plants off. My jeans are a little damp.

"I lost track of time," I say, rubbing my eyes.

I've been gone all day, and my stomach growls with hunger. I realize my parents are probably worried about me. Maybe I should go home first and—

"Are you ready?"

My breath catches in my throat. There's no time to go home. I can explain everything when I go back with Ingrid.

"Are—are we doing it here?" It feels so open and exposed, so unholy and wrong. But Ingrid is right below me.

"No, not here. We are going to the place where everything began. I think you know."

"The nature preserve?"

Artemis gives a single nod. Of course. The place where everything began—and ended.

"I brought my bike."

Artemis laughs, placing a hand on my shoulder.

"I'll make sure it finds its way home," she says. "We'll be going by a different method."

Artemis pulls a small bottle of gold liquid out of a hidden pocket in her cloak. It looks like one of the bottles I saw in her lab. She pulls out the cork stopper and tips the vial. The gold liquid spills out but doesn't hit the ground. Instead it spreads in a golden fog and envelops the two of us. Artemis grabs my wrist. I cough as it fills my nose and close my eyes. It smells like flowers, wet earth, and dead things. It smells like the salt of the ocean, like the cold of night. My feet leave the ground.

"Don't panic," Artemis says. "It will clear up in a second."

The graveyard drops away beneath me, Ingrid's gravestone becoming a tiny speck.

I'm flying.

More accurately, we're flying, and we're encased in a bubble with a thin golden sheen. I poke at it with my fingertip, but my finger passes right through the surface in a wisp of smoke, and I quickly pull my hand back. The sound of the bubble rushing through the air roars around us, like we're in a car speeding on the freeway.

"What is this?" I shout.

"Just a little magical transport I invented."

I watch the streets and houses pass below us, dotted with yellow lights. The tall towers of downtown Los Angeles cut the sky behind me. In front of me is the wide ocean, the orange glow of the sun dipping just below the horizon. Dozens of barges dot the water around the Port of Long Beach. The city sprawls out below, the neatly gridded squares of neighborhoods pushing up against the dark hills of Palos Verdes and the nature preserve.

The gates are locked at sunset, but that doesn't matter. We fly right over them. There are no lights on the paths. Dark shapes scuttle around, the nocturnal animals hiding from the strange shape coming out of the sky. A canyon cuts through the earth to the coast, dark water emptying into the ocean.

My stomach flips as we descend. It's like riding a roller coaster without a harness. My feet touch down on the dirt path, and I fall to my knees. The bubble dissolves into the dusk.

It takes a second for my head to stop spinning, but then I realize where we are. I recognize this spot. It is the lower path that runs along the creek, very close to the place where I fell.

Darkness descends quickly. The night air is full of the sounds of wildlife—owls hooting, coyotes and mice rustling through the underbrush, the ocean crashing in the near distance. The sounds of the city are far away.

"What do you need me to do?"

"Nothing," Artemis says. She reaches into her cloak—it must either be magical or have a million hidden pockets—and starts pulling out the supplies one by one. "I'll let you know when it's ready."

I watch her as she kneels to draw symbols in the dirt path. I can't quite make them out in the darkness. My ears and lips are cold, so I pull up the hood over my head and bounce on the balls of my feet. I hate waiting.

Artemis begins to pile the materials on top of the symbols. It looks more like an ancient ritual than a science experiment. I kick myself for not bringing my notebook and taking notes. I was too excited to think of it. She mumbles each ingredient under her breath.

"Sulphur…ammonium…saltpeter…"

Finally, when all the ingredients are in the circle, she stands up and turns to me.

"One last thing. Do you have what I asked you to bring?"

I pull the mint tin out of my pocket. I can still smell the remnants of spearmint when I flip open the lid. The moonlight casts the fragile gossamer wings in a pale light. Even in shadow, the Palos Verdes Blue is beautiful.

I step to the pile of chemicals that will make up Ingrid's new body and gently place the stiff butterfly on top. I'm sure Dad won't mind—he'd rather have Ingrid back than a butterfly. It might not be Ingrid's perfect specimen, but I hope that the symbolism is enough. I wonder if Mateo would be proud of me for thinking of a literary term.

Artemis produces a plastic jug of water, and I'm convinced fully that the cloak is magic.

"This is the final step," she says. "Be ready."

"Ready for what?" My voice is barely a whisper. It feels wrong to speak loudly here where the only sounds are from nature.

"To use your power," she says. "On my count."

My power has appeared in so many different ways, from the sprouts on my pencil to the flowers erupting under my footsteps. But can I control it? I think about my backyard and the way the vines tried to strangle me.

"Three."

I take a deep breath and think about the hours spent at Mateo's house. I can do this.

"Two."

I crouch down. The sounds of the wildlife are drowned out by the crashing of my heart against my chest. I imagine it's the waves crashing rhythmically against the shore.

"One."

I plunge my fingers into the gritty pile of elements just as

Artemis tips the jug. Water splashes onto my sneakers and pants. My hands are drenched.

The magic courses through me. In Mateo's room it was gentle and easy, like humming the tune of a song. Tonight, it's more like screaming at the top of my lungs. The magic pours out of me, not just through my fingers but through my whole body, leaving me lightheaded and empty. My vision blurs. I don't know what I expected—I thought there might be a bright white light, or that Ingrid would form in front of me as if she were made of clay. But her making is nothing like that. It feels more like I'm being *un*made. I feel pulled apart, like part of me is coming loose at the edges. The world sways around me, and I fall. The last thing I see is the moon above me, and then darkness.

Chapter 13

I wake up to dull, gray light. My head aches and my eyes are crusted with sleep. Was it all a dream? But no—I sit up in my own bed. I'm still wearing my sweatshirt, and the empty mint tin is in the front pocket. It was real.

I jump out of bed and dash down the stairs toward the smell of breakfast. I skid to a stop at the kitchen door.

Dad stands at the stove with a pan full of sizzling bacon and eggs. Mom sits at the table, a steaming mug of coffee in one hand and the morning news on her tablet in the other.

And beside her—beautifully, impossibly—is Ingrid.

She's wearing her pajamas, a pink striped camisole over baggy plaid pants. Her long blond hair is pulled back in a ponytail to keep it out of her clear blue eyes. Those blue eyes look up from the book in her hands and land on me.

Her smile is brilliant. It's wonderful. It's alive. I want to throw my arms around her and never let her go. I wonder how my parents are resisting—after two years of Ingrid being gone, how can they act like this is any other morning?

"Good morning," Ingrid says, setting the book down.

"Look who finally woke up," Dad says from the stove.

Mom looks up and smiles but doesn't say anything. How can they be so calm about this? Doubt creeps into my mind. I slide into my chair at the breakfast table. There are four chairs—Dad's is on my left, Mom's across from mine. Ingrid's is always on my right. Even when she was gone, her chair sat empty. But now it's full of her, and her presence is overwhelming. She gives me a knowing look, a mischievous twinkle in her eyes.

"Isn't this great?" I say, breaking the silence.

Mom and Dad both look over at me. Mom gives me a hesitant smile.

"Of course," Mom says slowly. "It's nice having breakfast together."

Dad brings us each a plate loaded with bacon and eggs. Everyone starts eating, but I stare at Ingrid. I can't take my eyes off her.

"You okay, June?" Dad says through a cheek full of egg.

"Yeah, I'm fine." I don't feel fine. I thought there would be more of a reaction to Ingrid being back. But they're acting like she's never been gone.

Ingrid finishes her eggs and downs a glass of orange juice.

"I'm going to get dressed," she says.

I leave my breakfast on the table and follow her. When we reach the upstairs hallway, she stops and turns to me. She smiles bigger than I've ever seen her smile before.

"Juniper," she says.

I throw my arms around her then, my eyes burning with tears I can't hold back. I sob silently into her shoulder, not wanting our parents to hear. She pats my back gently.

"It's okay," she says. "This will take time getting used to. I'm still getting used to it too."

I pull away, wiping my eyes on the sleeve of my sweatshirt.

"I don't understand," I whisper. "What happened last night? How come Mom and Dad are acting like…"

"Like I never left?"

She peeks down the stairs, then grabs my arm and pulls me into her room. Once the door is closed, she explains.

"I don't understand everything either," Ingrid says. She looks down at her hands, as if they are brand new to her. "When I woke up in the dirt, I was so confused. But a woman, Artemis, told me who I was. Ingrid. That's my name—Ingrid Edwards. I started to remember, bit by bit. It's still fuzzy. I stayed up all night, remembering."

Her eyes flicker up to me.

"I remember you're my sister." She grabs my hands and squeezes them, and I squeeze back.

I want to ask her how she died. I want to tell her about Artemis, and magic, and the stone in my pocket that made everything happen. My hands shake. I realize that she's taller than me—the height she would have been if she'd lived until high school. She looks older than I remember, but just like I imagined she would.

"There's so much I want to ask," I say, my voice choked.

"There will be time for questions later," she says. "But for now, we don't want to be late for school. I have a feeling that if we act like things are strange, it'll be harder for us. I'm guessing there's a lot you haven't told Mom and Dad."

I look at my feet. She's right. Right now, Mom and Dad don't even remember that Ingrid died. If we act weird about it, there will be even more questions. I take a deep breath.

"We need a plan," I say. "You're in high school now. Do you even know how to get there? What classrooms to go to?"

"Look at this."

She holds up a backpack and leans against her bed. It's dirty and baby blue, the same one I remember her using two years before. She slides out a binder. In the front clear cover is paper with a list of teacher's names and room numbers. It looks just like the one I have in my binder, but with one exception: at the top it has the name of the high school.

"But how?"

Ingrid shrugs.

"Artemis said she would take care of everything," she says.

"You know more about it than me, don't you? The magic?"

My heart lurches at the word. Magic. What do I know about magic? After last night, it feels like I don't really know anything at all.

The stone is still in my pocket. I pull it out—but it doesn't glow. The green is gone. It's a normal, pale gray rock with a swirled pattern like a snail's shell. I shake it, but the glow doesn't return. It stays dull.

"What's that?" Ingrid asks, cocking her head to the side.

"It's my magic." I hold it out for her to look at. "It's usually glowing."

"Is it broken?"

"I...I don't know," I say. "Magic is still new to me."

I put the stone back in my pocket, hoping Ingrid can't hear the panic in my voice. The stone's never done this before. I'll have to ask Artemis about it later.

"Let's not worry about it," I say. "Let's just focus on getting through school."

"Girls!" Dad's voice echoes from downstairs. "You ready?"

"Coming!" We shout it together, our voices harmonizing. We share a look and giggle. I'd forgotten our voices could do that. We're two years apart, but we've always been, as Dad says, two wings to the same butterfly.

I'm braced for the worst at school, but everyone's moved on from gossiping about me. I'm old news. At the beginning of each class, my teachers accept the late work I completed, and I sit down and listen as if nothing has happened at all. Even Mr. Harris doesn't give me a hard time. I guess Mom must have convinced him I had a medical emergency, because he gives me a small smile when I hand in my makeup test.

"Glad you're feeling better, Juniper," he says.

I look at my feet, still embarrassed about what happened. The potted plant on his desk still looks more vibrant than it had before. The magic has staying power. A chill goes through me when I remember the stone's dullness. I pause at his desk and gently touch a leaf of the plant. I imagine the plant sprouting vines that crawl across the floor and up the whiteboard. But nothing happens.

"Something wrong?" Mr. Harris asks, one eyebrow cocked in confusion.

I shake my head and take my seat. I stare out the window, hypotheticals turning in my head. Is magic limited? Did I use it all up last night? I didn't read anything like that in the book, but there's so much I don't know.

Mateo slides into the desk in front of me and breaks my focus.

"Hey." He smiles at me, which surprises me. How can he be nice to me after our fight on Saturday?

"I wanted to say sorry," he says. "I didn't mean to upset you. I was just...surprised."

The bell rings before I have a chance to respond. Mr. Harris calls everyone to their seats.

"Do you want to sit together at lunch?" Mateo asks quietly.

Maybe Mateo changed his mind. Maybe, like my parents, he also thinks Ingrid never died. I want to be mad at him for not believing Ingrid could come back, but it's hard to be mad when I was right.

I don't need friends. I have Ingrid. But Ingrid isn't here right now, so I nod. Maybe everything is okay after all.

English passes uneventfully, and not even PE puts me in a bad mood. I feel good. Ingrid's back, and Mateo doesn't hate me. When I walk into science class, I know that everything is going to be all right.

Chelsea is already seated at her lab table with her two friends. She has a ridiculously large bow in her hair with mustaches printed on it. I roll my eyes. I will never understand fashion.

When she spots me, the trio stops giggling. They watch me walk into the room and sit down at my own lab table. Even though they are behind me, I can feel their eyes on my back. A moment later, Chelsea's at my side.

"Did you finish the project?" she asks.

"Of course I did." I slide the rolled-up poster out of my backpack, and she sighs, relieved.

"You're the best, June," she says. Normally that would bother me. "June" is what she called me when we were friends, and we're not now. It feels wrong to hear her say it. But I smile, because it

160

doesn't matter. She can call me June all she likes.

She sits back down at her lab table and class begins. Mrs. Cartwright calls groups up one by one. Unsurprisingly, everyone's projects are dull. Good enough for seventh grade life science, maybe, but none of them are scientists like me. They barely cite their sources, and when they do, they're from the science textbook. Amateurs. My project—I mean, our project— has references from six academic journals. Being the daughter of a college professor has its perks.

My mind wanders during the dull presentations, thinking about all the research Ingrid and I can do together now. Before she died, I barely knew anything about science. Now Dad says I'm keener than some of his college students. With our skills combined, I'm sure we'll catch a Palos Verdes Blue in no time.

Finally, Mrs. Cartwright calls Chelsea and me to the front.

"You talk about all the science parts, and I'll talk about everything else," Chelsea whispers.

I shrug. Chelsea doesn't know that our project is pretty much all science now, like it should be. It's science class, not art class, and I want to get an A.

I unroll the poster and clip it to top of the white board. The class stares at us, bored as always on presentation day, but I hear Chelsea give a little gasp when she sees our project. I think she's going to say something, but she doesn't. She just bites her lip and stares at it. The ponytails on each side of her head make her look like a baby.

"Plants and Animals of the Palos Verdes Nature Preserve," I begin, reading the title that's still printed in Chelsea's block letters. "Also known as flora and fauna…"

I go through every section, trying my best to recite from memory. Dad says you should never read straight from the presentation, so I try to summarize. The other kids still look bored, but they just don't appreciate science. Mrs. Cartwright looks interested, and every once in a while she looks down and marks a comment on her grade sheet.

Chelsea stands silently through the whole presentation. When I'm finished talking, I look at her. She gestures to the bottom, where I re-pasted the pictures of her and her friends.

"These are some pictures from the nature preserve," she says. Her voice is shaking. For a second I feel bad for her—but it's not my fault she didn't write any of the actual science parts. It's not my fault that she wanted to treat this like an art project.

She points to each picture and describes it briefly, but the usual bubbly tone is gone from her voice. When she's done, the class claps disinterestedly.

"Thank you, girls," Mrs. Cartwright says. "That was a very… well-researched presentation."

I grin. I knew that I made the right call by changing everything. Chelsea should be thanking me for saving our grade and putting so much work into the project. But instead she stomps back to her seat and doesn't look at me. I unclip the poster and add it to the pile on Mrs. Cartwright's desk.

Chelsea and her friends are whispering at their lab table while Mrs. Cartwright ruffles through her papers to decide who should go next. Out of the corner of my eye I see them glare at me. But I'm not worried. I know we just got an A.

When the bell rings, Mateo and I walk to the cafeteria together. His curls bob up and down beside me.

"Your project was great!" he says. "You used so many words I didn't even know existed."

"You know poetry. I know science. Everyone has their thing," I say. I feel like I'm floating as we make our way down the hall.

"I wonder if I could make a poem out of scientific words..." Mateo looks up dreamily and almost crashes into an eighth grader. I pull him out of the way just in time.

"That could be neat," I say. "Some of the words are really pretty."

We grab trays and get in line.

"Like what?"

"Well, the first one I can think of is lepidoptera," I say, wrinkling my nose at the soggy green beans.

"What's that one mean?"

"Butterflies," I say. "And also moths."

"Huh."

Mateo ponders this as we carry our trays to a lunch table in the corner. It's the wobbly one, so no one likes to sit there, but if we each sit on one side it stays steady.

"Tell me another one," Mateo says.

I take a bite of rectangular pizza—it's still a little cold in the middle—and think about it.

"Okay, how about Anisoptera?"

"What's that one mean? Wait, let me guess…it ends with the same sound as lepidoptera, so it must be related…"

Mateo takes a thoughtful sip of chocolate milk. I never thought to play word games with scientific terms, but it's actually fun.

Before Mateo can answer, I feel someone standing behind me.

"What do you want?" Mateo says over my shoulder, frowning.

I'm surprised at his tone, so I turn around. Chelsea and her two friends surround me. Chelsea has a hand on her hip, and the other two have their arms crossed.

"You ruined our project," Chelsea says.

"I did not." How could I have ruined it? I saved it. She should be thanking me.

"All my drawings!" she shrieks. "You covered them all up! And moved my photos! You made it so boring!"

The word *boring* made my heart beat loud in my ears.

"Our project was not boring," I say, trying to keep my voice steady. "Mrs. Cartwright loved it."

"She did not! No one even knows what you were talking about." She waves her arms angrily. "Just because you used bigger words didn't make it better."

"She said it was well-researched," I say. "You didn't even do any research!"

"But I spent hours on those drawings!"

People around us are starting to stare. Normally I would just turn around and put my head down and ignore Chelsea. I don't want to be seen having a fight in the cafeteria. I like it better when I'm invisible. But I imagine Ingrid at my side, telling me to defend myself. I imagine Ingrid a lot, but now that she's back, I feel her strength as if she's sitting right next to me.

"Save your doodles for art class, Chelsea. In science we do diagrams. Don't be mad at me because you didn't put any effort into the group project and left all the hard work for me, like you always do."

I turn back around, not wanting to look at Chelsea's stupid face or outfit anymore. I take another bite of rectangle pizza, trying to look casual. Mateo smiles at me, eyes wide, and it feels nice to have a friend that's on my side for once.

"I don't care if you and your sister want to be weirdo science freaks, but if you ruin my art again, you're going to regret it."

The mention of Ingrid makes my heart jump in my chest. Does Chelsea know that Ingrid is alive? Is Artemis's magic working on her, just like it worked on my parents?

"Hey!" Mateo shouts at her. "You shouldn't talk about her sister like that."

"What, do you have a crush on her or something?" Chelsea scoffs.

Mateo's eyebrows crease together, like he's confused.

Their footsteps shuffle away, and Mateo and I are left alone.

"That was a low blow, for her to bring up your sister like that," he says quietly. "It must be really hard, losing a sibling."

Mateo doesn't meet my eyes, but I stare at him.

Mom, Dad, Chelsea...they think Ingrid is alive. But not Mateo. He picks at his food, looking gloomy. Why did everyone else forget, but not him? It doesn't make any sense.

We eat the rest of our lunch in silence. I will have to tell him the truth. Even though he was against it, he can't be mad now that it actually worked, can he? But then Mateo starts talking about a writing camp he went to over the summer, and the moment passes.

The rest of the day passes uneventfully, but my good mood has evaporated. Mateo finds me near the front of the school after the last bell while everyone floods out into the warm afternoon sun. I know I should tell him that Ingrid is alive, but I don't know how.

As we walk out of school, he chatters about something that happened during seventh period, but I'm not really listening. We're crossing the big grass field in front of the school when I hear my name.

"Juniper!"

I turn around, and there she is. Ingrid. Her hair is pulled back into a sporty ponytail, and she has her backpack slung over her shoulder. She waves at me from the other side of the grass and starts walking toward me.

"Who's that?" Mateo asks.

"It's, um…well, I've been meaning to tell you…"

Ingrid closes the gap between us. Mateo's eyes widen. Ingrid looks a lot like me—same blue eyes, though her hair's blond and mine's brown. Her face is longer, and so are her legs, but we are undeniably siblings.

"Hey, June." Ingrid ruffles my hair. "Hope you don't mind walking home with your sister today."

That's it. There's no denying it now. I look back at Mateo. His shock has turned into something else. His eyebrows are knitted together, like he's thinking really hard about something. He looks almost…angry?

I should have told him sooner. I should have explained everything. But I didn't, and now he knows anyway. The three of us stand there in an awkward silence.

"I wanted to tell you—"

"Don't bother." I've never heard Mateo sound like that before. He turns around and stomps in the opposite direction, directly into the crowd of students.

"Mateo! Wait!"

But he doesn't wait. He's gone.

"Who was that?" Ingrid asks.

I stare into the crowd, looking desperately for his curly brown hair, but I don't see it anywhere.

If Mateo is mad about this, then fine. I don't need friends anyway. I have Ingrid, and that's all that matters. Everything is perfect now. Mateo was wrong, and I was right.

"No one important," I say. I grab Ingrid's hand and pull her away.

Chapter 14

Ingrid skips and hums as we walk home. This is something I've never seen her do before, but maybe this second chance at life has changed her attitude. She giggles at every car that drives by.

"Green one!" she shouts, pointing as a big green SUV zooms past. Right behind it is a speedy black sports car. "Black one!"

It's weird, but I can't help but laugh at how excited she is. They probably don't have cars in...wherever you go when you're dead. I want to ask her about it, but she's so happy, and I don't want to ruin it. I push Mateo and Chelsea out of my mind.

When we turn on our street, Ingrid looks up at the Elm House and gasps. She grabs on to the wrought iron bars of the front gate and stares at it.

"Whoa. This one is different from all the others."

"Do you remember it?" I ask. "It looked abandoned before I got magic."

Ingrid shakes her head.

"Everything is still fuzzy," she says.

"We'll figure it out," I say. "Artemis lives there."

Ingrid's eyes sparkle as she takes it all in—the beautiful gardens, the brightly painted walls, the tower with the cone-shaped roof.

"We should go see her," I say. "She'll want to examine you."

"How do we get in?" Ingrid asks, shaking the bars of the gate. "It's locked."

"There's a secret way. I'll show you."

We leave our backpacks on our front porch, and I lead Ingrid to the gap in the bushes. We get down on our hands and knees and crawl through the fence. She gasps when we emerge in the garden.

"This is amazing." Her voice is a whisper as she looks at the hedge rows and the carefully trimmed rosebushes.

"The garden is Soren's," I say. "He's probably around some-where."

"Is he magic, like Artemis?"

I give Ingrid a sidelong smile.

"You'll see."

I lead Ingrid up to the front door of the Elm House and lift the dragon knocker. It's fun being the one to reveal magical secrets for once. Even though it's Artemis who opens the door, I feel like I'm the one parting the curtain.

Artemis stands before us, her hair pulled up in its usual messy bun. She's wearing a dark blue cloak over her loose black clothes and heavy boots. Her gloves have dark spots of ash on them. She pulls them off and steps aside from the door.

"Juniper! What a pleasant surprise. Do come in."

She peels off her cloak and hangs it on the coatrack next to the door. Ingrid stops in the doorway. Her eyes light up at the rich carpet and elegant paintings on the walls. She looks at the painting at the top of the stairs for several moments, then glances back down at Artemis, making the connection right away.

"This is...wow."

"Welcome to Elm House," Artemis says, gesturing around with her hands. "There will time for the tour later, I believe. For now, we should get better acquainted. I do believe our first introduction was under inauspicious circumstances. Ingrid, isn't it?"

Ingrid nods, speechless. Artemis holds out a hand, and Ingrid shakes it.

"I've heard much about you, and I'm sure you've heard about me. I'm Artemis Alderdice. Now come, sit, let's have some tea."

Artemis leads us into the room with the piano, then leaves to fetch the tea. Sunlight fills the room, cast green from the garden just beyond the windows. I sit beside Ingrid on the fancy, old-fashioned couch, the one where I first told Artemis that I wanted to bring Ingrid back to life. And here she is. A promise fulfilled.

"Hello, there."

A familiar voice echoes from above. I look up, and Soren is hanging from the chandelier with one hand. He drops onto the floor in front of us, and Ingrid lets out a little yelp. Soren stands upright on his hind legs, gives a slight bow, then holds a hand out to Ingrid.

"The name's Soren," he says. "You must be Ingrid."

Ingrid looks at me with wide blue eyes, then takes his hand and gently shakes it.

"It's nice to meet you," she says. "You have such a lovely garden."

Soren inclines his head modestly. "I'll have to give you a tour sometime."

Artemis comes in with a pot of tea and three teacups on a tray. She places it on the coffee table. Soren jumps on top of the piano, curling up like a cat and watching us with wide eyes.

Artemis bends down, looking Ingrid directly in the eyes. I hear Ingrid's breath catch as Artemis takes her chin in her fingers, turning her head left and right.

"Fascinating," Artemis breathes.

She pokes and prods Ingrid, lifting her arms and feeling her pulse before stepping back.

"Forgive me," she says. "I am simply admiring Juniper's handiwork. And I must say, you are incredible. Completely indistinguishable from a natural-born human."

"What do you mean?" I ask. "She's not…human?"

"Well, I suppose that depends on your definition of human," Artemis says. "Is it our bodies that make us human? If so, then she is perfectly human in every way. It's not the same body that was born from your mother, no, but it is a human body nonetheless, one that you created."

Ingrid looks at me, and I feel my heart swell. One that I created. She's back because of me. Maybe it's not her same exact body, but it's *her*, and that's what matters.

"Artemis, no one seems to remember Ingrid died, not even my parents," I say. "How is that possible?"

"Magic is all about how one perceives the world," Artemis explains. "People tend to see what they want to see. I concocted a glamour on Ingrid. It's a magical way of changing what people can see. It's the same sort of magic that I use on the house, but a bit more complicated. This glamour works on the minds of those who around her. No one wants to believe she's dead, of course, so they see what they want to see: a teenage girl who is bright, healthy, and very much *alive*."

I think about what Artemis told me the first time I came here: half of magic is the wanting. Does wanting something hard enough make it real?

Artemis finishes her examination of Ingrid, looking pleased.

"You have proven yourself a strong and adept magician, Juniper," she says. "Now that the experiment to bring back Ingrid was successful, I must remind you of your promise to help me."

"Of course," I say. "Anything."

I hope that Artemis doesn't hear my hesitation. I want to ask her about my stone—why it's stopped glowing, whether the magic is fading—but I don't want her to change her mind about letting me help.

"Most excellent," Artemis says, clapping her hands together. "I would like to start right away, but I ran into an old acquaintance when I was in Santa Monica, and they've asked me to help them with an enchantment tomorrow evening. Then, of course, I must go through the old notes, and I'm sure you'll want some time to settle in. Come back next week, will you? And Ingrid, I do hope you will join us."

"Sure!" Ingrid says, nodding enthusiastically.

We say goodbye to Artemis and Soren and make our way back through the garden to our own yard. At our front door, I look back at the lawn, where my shoes made imprints on the grass. No flowers. Still no magic.

"What do you remember about science?" I ask Ingrid as we kick off our shoes.

"Not much," she says. "We're doing chemical equations in chemistry class."

"Come look at this." I lead her into the den and turn on the light. Ingrid gasps as she looks around at all the cases of butterflies and insects that line the walls. She runs up to one that houses the moths Dad caught on a research trip to South America and puts her face so close to the glass that it fogs up from her breath.

"Are these real?"

"They're real," I say. "We used to catch them together. Do you remember?"

She moves from case to case, her forehead wrinkled in thought. A few of Dad's specimens are missing, but since they got mixed up when the cases broke, he hasn't noticed yet. Ingrid stops in front of her own case—the butterflies she caught before the accident. She narrows her eyes and lifts a finger to a pinned California Ringlet.

"*Coenonympha tullia california,*" she says, reading the label beneath it. "We caught this one on the hill behind the elementary school."

"Yes!"

The memory of that day floods into my mind. We weren't even there for butterflies. It was the school carnival. We spotted it while we were in line for the rock wall, and Ingrid and I chased it all the way across the field. We didn't have a net or bags or anything, so Ingrid carefully held it cupped in her hands. When Mom found us, accompanied by the principal, she wasn't happy. But Dad was proud of us for improvising.

Ingrid's finger slides across the glass at the others. Some she skips, and I can't fill in those memories—she caught them without me. But the others she remembers just as clearly as I do. When she gets to the bottom, her finger stops on the label for the Palos Verdes Blue. She frowns.

"This one. We never caught this one."

"Not yet," I say. "It's one of the rarest in the world. But I haven't given up."

I cross the room to Dad's desk. In the back of one of the drawers, dusty and ignored, are Ingrid's old field notebooks. I pull them out for her, and she begins to flip through them. There are pages and pages of notes and maps and sketches. She thumbs through them wordlessly, sometimes pausing on particular drawings or figures.

"I worked really hard on this," she says finally.

"I kept working on it, even after…" I swallow. "There was another notebook, but it got wet. I'm sorry."

"That's okay," Ingrid says. "There's plenty here. I remember…I remember the plants, and the air, and the ocean. Where did we make all this?"

"The nature preserve. Do you remember?"

Ingrid looks up at me, the book limp in her hands. She shakes her head.

"We rode our bikes there all the time," I tell her. "It's the only place the Blue is found in the wild. That's where we did our research."

She frowns again and looks past me, her eyes blank. I can tell she's thinking really hard.

"Something else about that place feels familiar."

I let out a long breath. I have to tell her the truth.

"It's where you died."

Ingrid's bike is in the garage with the other bikes. Mom wanted to sell it, but Dad thought it would be good to keep in case anything happened to mine. I'm glad they kept it. It's dusty and the tires are flat, but other than that, it works fine. I fill the tires with the air pump and find an extra helmet for Ingrid. She shoves it awkwardly over her hair and looks skeptically at the bike.

"You remember how to ride it, right?" I wheel mine down the driveway, and she mimics me. "They say you never forget how."

"Who says?"

It occurs to me that I don't know who says that, and that whoever they are probably didn't test that claim scientifically.

I climb on and pedal slowly at first, so Ingrid can copy me. She has a few false starts, but after a minute she's riding down our street as smoothly as a fish glides through water. Wind fills my ears as we pedal down the hills toward the nature preserve. I look back every few seconds to make sure Ingrid is okay. Every time I do, she's not looking ahead of her, but all around, like she's a tourist in her own neighborhood.

We turn a corner, and the ocean comes into view, and Ingrid stops. I brake, then turn around and wheel my bike back to where she's standing.

"Everything okay?"

"Yeah, just...I didn't remember."

Ingrid's eyes glitter with the reflection of the blue sky and the wide expanse of water. The sky is clear, though there's a bit of haze on the horizon. Large barges move slowly in the distance.

"What's that?"

Ingrid points at a large, looming brown mass. It's fuzzy from here—it looks like a jagged mountain jutting out of the water.

"That's Catalina Island," I say.

"Oh, right." She blinks, as if coming out of a dream, then smiles at me. "I can't believe I forgot about the ocean."

"Come on," I say. "Let's see what else you can remember."

We ride our bikes through the open gate into the nature preserve. Our tires bump over the dirt path. With Ingrid beside me, I'm reminded of all the times we came here together. She would lead me down the right paths and tell me the scientific names of all the plants. Now I'm the one leading her.

I pause by a cluster of bush sunflowers. A fat honeybee buzzes around the petals. Ingrid stands beside me—I can hear her breathing, and the feeling gives me chills. She giggles as she watches the bee bop around and fly away.

"*Encelia Californica*," I say. "Do you remember?"

She tips her head to one side and leans in to smell one of the flowers.

"They don't smell like much," she says.

"Let's find some purple sage."

We continue down the path, ignoring the educational sign-posts that talk about the animals and the tides. The path turns downward, and we have to hold tight to our bikes so they don't

178

roll away. If we follow this path long enough it'll take us to the beach, but instead we turn to the right. The path narrows here. It's less popular among humans, which means it's more popular among the local fauna. Ingrid and I spent most of our time on these out-of-the-way paths.

I watch her as we walk. She looks all around, her eyes drinking in the plants, the ocean, the sky. Then suddenly she stops. Her face falls, and she stares out into the distance.

I stop too, and I realize where we are. We are next to the creek where I fell but on the other side. I can see the path my classmates took when we went on our field trip and the spot where Artemis staged the experiment. It's strange to see it from the other side of the canyon, to see it from a different perspective.

Ingrid's forehead is creased again as she stares down at the water. While she's distracted, I pull the stone out of my pocket. If this is where everything happened, if this is where magic is, then my stone would work here—if it's going to work at all. But it's still dull.

Ingrid takes her helmet off. Her hair sticks to her forehead. I take mine off too, and the cool ocean breeze feels good against my damp skin. We stare at the creek and listen to it murmur across the rocks. It's not nearly as deep now as it was before, but I don't want to get close enough to see.

"There's something I've been wanting to ask you." I take a deep breath. "Do you remember what happened that night?"

Ingrid does not ask which night I am talking about. She

shakes her head.

"I'm sorry." Her voice is a whisper, nearly lost in the wind. "I don't remember. I know that it happened, but…I don't remember how or why."

I don't know what I was expecting Ingrid to say. I hoped she'd have answers, but now I have more questions than before. How come she can't remember anything? Did I mess up somehow?

A dragonfly flits past, and Ingrid's attention snags on it. We watch it land gently on the water, then it flies up and into a bush of purple sage on the other side of the creek.

"*Salvia leucophylla*," Ingrid says.

"You remember!"

She turns to me and grins. "Little by little."

There are a lot of things I don't understand, but I've never let that stop me before. Science doesn't stop with the experiment—I still need to collect and analyze the data. I'm missing a few data points with Ingrid, but as we stand together in the nature preserve, I have a feeling that I'll get them as long as she stays by my side.

PART V

Analyze

Chapter 15

The next week blurs together. I feel better than I have in a long time. From the moment I open my eyes, happiness bubbles in my chest. It's what I imagine winning the Nobel Prize would be like. Everything I've worked for has paid off. Ingrid is here, and she is alive, and everything is perfect.

When I'm at school, I talk to no one, trying my best to keep my head down and get my work done. But after school, Ingrid and I do everything together. We sneak ice cream from the freezer. We watch movies that Ingrid doesn't remember, including one of my favorites: *A Bug's Life*. And of course, we ride our bikes down to the nature preserve and spend hours looking for insects. I'm excited to go back to the Elm House and start experimenting, but I also like when it's just Ingrid and me. I haven't tried to do any magic, and the stone in my pocket stays gray. No signs of green light whatsoever. I log this observation in my journal, but I don't think too much about it. Ingrid takes up most of my thoughts.

Ingrid's scientific knowledge is lacking, and she is much less matter-of-fact than she was before she died, but I figure she just needs time to adjust. She's started carrying around Mom's old digital camera for observations. When we go to the nature preserve, she's less focused on finding the Blue and more focused on getting a perfect shot of the sun setting over the water. Sunsets are probably more beautiful after you haven't seen them for two years. I'm sure she'll come around after the novelty wears off.

One day after school, I decide to show her the tools Dad keeps at his desk for butterfly collecting. We haven't caught anything yet, but I want to get Ingrid up to speed. She doesn't seem to remember any of them.

"This is the setting board." I point to a long white board. Ingrid's camera goes "click."

"This is the relaxing box." I point to a clear box with a thick sponge lining. "Insects can be stiff, so relaxing them makes it easier to adjust them for mounting."

"Like a little insect spa?" Ingrid asks, pointing the camera at the box.

"Um. No. They're dead already. Relaxing is when you use vinegar and water to make their bodies softer. That way, they're less likely to break when you pin them."

"Oh." Her face falters. "After you catch them, how do they die, exactly? Do you just wait for them to die of old age?"

"Some people do that, but then their wings look tattered, so that's not great for collection." I reach up to a shelf above Dad's desk and pull down a jar. "This is the killing jar."

"That sounds so intense." She points her camera at the jar in my hands. Click.

"It's not that intense," I say. "See this plaster bottom? You pour the killing agent inside, and it goes under the plaster. You put the insect inside with some crumpled-up paper, and they perch on that until the fumes from the chemical kills them. We usually use ethyl acetate, but Dad keeps it locked up with the other chemicals."

Ingrid frowns as I explain this.

"Taking insects out of their habitat seems bad enough," she says. "Don't you feel bad killing them?"

My hands falter, and I set the jar on the desk. My chest feels tight. Ingrid has killed dozens of insects, even mounted many of the specimens on these walls herself. But she looks at me now, her forehead wrinkled, as if it disgusts her.

"Don't you remember any of this?" I ask.

"A little," she says.

"Ingrid, you were the one who taught me how to do this."

Ingrid looks away from the killing jar, her face crumpled.

"I'm sorry," she says. "I don't remember."

I remember the way she explained the killing agent to me,

how to measure out just the right amount. I remember her holding her hand over mine as I held the pin and set my very first specimen. Never once before did she question the ethics of insect collection—she'd always say, confidently, "It's for science."

"I know what we can do instead," she says suddenly. "We can take a selfie!"

"What?" The statement catches me off-guard, but before I can respond, she grabs me around the shoulders and turns the lens of the camera toward us. The flash goes off before I can adjust my face, and then she turns the screen around to show me.

"You look so serious!" She giggles.

It's weird seeing myself in a picture with Ingrid after all these years. She's taller, and she wears her hair in a big bun on the top of her head, which she never did before. And she's right—I do look serious. My eyes are wide and startled, and my mouth is in a weird twist, not quite smiling and not quite frowning. I've never liked taking photos of myself.

A loud ping sounds. I look around.

"What was that?" I ask.

"Oh!" Ingrid reaches into her pocket and pulls out a cell phone.

"You have a cell phone?" I ask.

"Mom gave it to me yesterday, since I'm in high school now. Jealous?" She hip checks me, and I grab the desk to keep my balance.

"I'm not jealous," I say, annoyed. I wait while Ingrid taps something out on her phone. "I was thinking we could go try to catch something. For practice, even if it's not the Blue. There were a lot of Common Ringlets last time we were out, or maybe a Hairstreak—"

"I can't." Ingrid doesn't look up, still tapping. "Lucy wants to hang out. I promised her I would."

"Lucy? Who's Lucy?"

"She's in my history class. She helped me out in class, and then we started eating lunch together." Ingrid looks up and beams. "Aren't you proud of me, June? I made a friend!"

"But what about the butterflies?" I gesture to the equipment laid out across the desk. "What about finding the Blue?"

What about me?

"The butterflies will still be there tomorrow." She puts her new cell phone into her pocket. "Besides, it's nice having a friend. It makes me feel normal. Like I fit in."

"But we were going to the nature preserve together," I say. "I can't just go alone."

"We've been there every day this week," she groans. "You don't have to go alone. You don't have to go at all. Do something else."

"I don't want to do something else!" I clench my fists, my voice rising. "I want to collect specimens with you!"

"Well, I don't want to!" Ingrid raises her voice to match mine. "I want to do something other than science for once!"

Ingrid's words echo strangely in my ears. Other than science? *Other than science*? Ingrid was always the one who loved field-work. She was always going off on her bike, and I had to beg her to take me along. And now she doesn't want to go at all?

I'm shaking too hard to respond. I turn around and run out of the den. I hear Ingrid's voice shouting behind me, but I don't listen. I run up the stairs and slam my door behind me.

There is something not right with Ingrid. She's supposed to like science, not taking selfies and hanging out with friends. That's never what she did before. At this rate, we will never find the Blue.

I have to get Ingrid interested in science again. Maybe going back to the Elm House to work on Artemis's new experiment will help. Surely when she sees what Artemis can do, she'll want to study them further. All I have to do is show her the possibilities, and then she'll be curious, focused Ingrid again. She'll act the way Ingrid should.

I run downstairs just as Ingrid is putting on her shoes.

"I'm sorry," I say. "I shouldn't have gotten mad."

Ingrid stands and pulls me into an awkward hug.

"It's okay," she says. "There'll be plenty of time to go bug catching."

"Do you want to go to the Elm House tomorrow?" I ask. "Artemis told us to come back this week. Maybe she'll be ready for us to help with her new experiment."

Ingrid's phone pings again, and she pulls it out of her pocket.

"Sure," she says, looking down at the screen. "Sounds good. See you later, June."

She opens the front door and heads toward a blue car I've

never seen before. There are already three other teenage girls in it, and they're looking down at the glowing screens in their laps as Ingrid skips across the front lawn toward them.

I don't understand. What does she need friends for? She has me.

Something catches my eye in the grass, in the footprints Ingrid leaves behind. She gets into the car, and it zooms away, but I can't stop staring at the lawn. Inside the outlines of her shoes are dozens of small, white flowers.

Ingrid doesn't get back until late, after I've already fallen asleep, so I don't get a chance to ask her about what happened. The grass. The flowers. The magic. I don't know how it's possible. Does she even know that it's happening? I have so many new questions. I need to talk to Artemis.

Ingrid's not interested in talking about it the next morning, though. She sleeps in late, and when she finally does wake up, she breezes through the kitchen and out the door. Her new high school friends are driving her to school.

I walk to school by myself. In English class, Mateo still won't talk to me. When Mr. Harris tells us to choose partners to analyze a poem, Mateo moves quickly across the classroom to pair up with someone else. The boy I get stuck with texts the whole time, leaving me to do the analysis. The words jumble together more than ever. No matter how hard I try, I can't stop thinking about the small white flowers in Ingrid's footprints.

My mood lifts slightly when I get to science class and see a stack of pen-covered papers on Mrs. Cartwright's desk. We get our project grades today. I'm ready to get a good grade and prove to Chelsea once and for all that science beats art.

Mrs. Cartwright comes around with the stack of papers. She places a paper facedown in front of me and says, "Good job."

I beam. This is it. I flip the paper over and my heart sinks. Written on the top, in red Sharpie marker, is the score 88.

A B? How could we get a B? Our project was the most thorough and well-researched of all of them. I scan the rubric. At the bottom of the score sheet it says, "Creativity: 70/100."

Creativity? On a science project? It takes all my willpower not to crumple up the paper and throw it across the room. I can't stomach reading the comments at the bottom. Instead I shove it into my backpack where I won't have to look at it. I don't dare turn around and look at Chelsea. Even though Mrs. Cartwright gives us each our own rubric, I know she got the same grade. If she was mad before, she'll be furious now.

For the rest of the class I can feel Chelsea's eyes burning into my back. When the bell rings, I'm the first one out the door.

The uneasy feelings churn in my stomach for the rest of day. Normally the thought of Ingrid would help me through a rough day like this, but I don't know if she'll even be waiting for me after school. She has high school friends now.

When we all stream out of the school, backpacks banging as

everyone tries to make it through the gate as quickly as possible, I see her on the sidewalk waiting for me. She smiles and waves, and relief washes over me.

"I had such an amazing day," Ingrid says. That makes one of us. As we walk home she rattles off all the things that happened—someone played a prank on one of the teachers, some other girl I've never heard of is going to be an extra on a TV show and promised to get Ingrid a spot, one of Ingrid's friends has a crush on some girl...

Ingrid talks so fast that it all jumbles together. I don't want to talk about high school and friends and crushes. I want to talk about science. I want to talk about magic. I want to talk about us. But I can't get a word in.

We're a few blocks away from school when someone tugs hard on my backpack. I spin around. There's Chelsea, arms crossed, a glare glued to her face. Ingrid stops talking mid-sentence.

"Is this your friend?" she asks, frowning.

Chelsea ignores her.

"It's your fault we didn't get an A on our project." She's so mad she's shaking, and the unfolded paperclips she uses as earrings wobble in her ears.

"If it wasn't for me, we would've gotten an F," I say.

"You covered up my drawings!" Chelsea's voice is shrill, but there's no one on this block to hear it except for me and Ingrid. She stomps her foot. "You moved all my pictures to the bottom!"

"Because it's a science project, not a scrapbook."

"Well, clearly Mrs. Cartwright doesn't think so, because we got a B!"

I try to turn away, but Chelsea yanks on my arm.

"We're not done talking about this!"

Ingrid shoves Chelsea hard on the shoulders. "Don't touch my sister."

Chelsea stumbles back. Her eyes dart nervously from Ingrid to me.

"What you did wasn't right," Chelsea says, voice wobbling. "If you wanted to do the project differently, you should've asked me first."

"Well, maybe you should've asked me before you covered our project in stupid drawings in the first place!"

Chelsea's face turns bright red.

"They're not stupid!" she shouts. "What is wrong with you lately? Anything that's not perfectly, exactly science-y is bad to you now. You used to be cool, but now you're a boring jerk!"

I clench my fists. I know that I am a lot more interested in science than other people, but it's not boring. Being called a jerk to my face stings.

"You take that back," I say.

"Or what? You'll have your sister beat me up? You're a jerk *and* a coward."

I'm so angry that I can hear my teeth grinding together.

"Don't talk to my sister that way!" Ingrid shouts. She puts a hand on my shoulder, and suddenly the world is spinning.

It feels like an electric shock. The jolt floods from Ingrid's hand to the top of my head and the tips of my toes. My vision is flushed with a green tint. I felt this way once before: the night I plunged my hands into the earth and brought Ingrid back to life.

My entire body pulses with menace and magic. How can Chelsea attack me like this when I did most of the work on the project? How can she be mad about me not talking with her after she made it clear that we are *not* friends anymore?

I open my mouth, ready to yell, but magic comes out instead of words. Vines shoot out from the cracks in the sidewalk below Chelsea's feet. They push through, breaking off bits of concrete as they rocket skyward. Chelsea's eyes widen as the vines wrap themselves around her legs, growing larger and tighter with every second. She screams as her feet leave the ground.

Ingrid's hand tightens on my shoulder. My breathing is heavy. I've never felt magic this powerful before. When I did magic in Mateo's room, I felt like a magical watering can, trickling water out so everything could grow. Now I feel like a hurricane—no gentle pitter-patter, just a wild, angry storm.

"I'm not a coward!" I scream. "It's not my fault we got a B. I saved our grade. I'm the one who fixed everything! Me! You're just mad because I'm smarter than you!"

Chelsea pushes at the thick vines that wrapped around her waist. Smaller vines whip up to grab her hands. I wait for some sort of snarky comeback, the kind she always sneered out to make me feel like I was lower than dirt. But it doesn't come.

When she looks up, her face is wet with tears.

Something inside me snaps.

What am I doing? I try to let go of the magic, but I haven't practiced enough—it's totally out of my control. I try to remember what Mateo taught me, about the waves crashing against the water, but there's too much chaos bouncing around in my head. It feels like a bad dream I can't wake up from.

"No," I choke, and I pull away just enough so Ingrid's grip on me breaks. The magic falls away, the vines shriveling to nothing, leaving only the broken sidewalk behind. Chelsea falls to her knees, her eyes wide, gasping small, panicked breaths.

I run over to Chelsea, apologies pouring out of me. But when I kneel to help her up, she swats me away.

"You're a psycho!" she sobs. "Get away from me!"

She picks herself up and runs unsteadily in the other direction.

Ingrid stares down at her hands, eyes wide with shock and horror.

"Did…did I…?"

I stand and wipe the sweat off my forehead. I'm drenched—using magic that strong felt like running the mile at school three times in a row. I can barely stand without feeling dizzy, and all my muscles ache. I lean on Ingrid to stay steady.

"That's the magic." I reach into my pocket and pull out the stone. The soft spiral curves are still dull and gray. Not a lick of green to them. "I don't know how, but when you touched me…I think it came out of you."

"What does it mean?" Ingrid's voice shakes.

"It'll be okay," I say. "Let's go talk to Artemis. She'll know what to do."

We walk slowly down the street. Something aches in me, and it isn't physical. The book said that magicians can channel their magic through an object. The stone was my object—but now it's lifeless, and Ingrid has magic. Is she a magician now? Or is it possible that she took the stone's place—*she's* the magic object? Either way, it's unfair. Ingrid, who isn't even interested in science now, has my magic power. I'm the one who nearly drowned for it. I'm the one who studied it. I should have it, not her.

Before, I wanted nothing more than to tell Ingrid about my day. But now, silence stretches between us.

Chapter 16

Ingrid isn't behind me as I crawl through the bushes to the Elm House.

"Ingrid?" I twist around to see her standing in our yard. "Are you coming?"

"My clothes will get all dirty."

"Since when do you care about that?" Ingrid used to wear stained jeans and oversized T-shirts. She was always convincing me to go off-trail for field research, through muddy paths and cobwebby shrubs. If Ingrid wasn't dirty, it was because she was home sick. Now that I look at her, though, I realize that her shirt clings to her body, and her jeans have rhinestones on them. Since when does she care about fashion?

After a moment of hesitation, she gets down on her hands

and knees with me. When we get to the other side, she takes great care dusting the soil off her jeans.

I let Ingrid lead the way to the Elm House's front door so I can look down at her footprints. The grass grows longer everywhere she steps, and the space fills with white-and-yellow flowers. This time Ingrid notices it too.

"Look!" she gasps. "The magic step!"

She runs in circles around the grass, drawing figure eights out of magic flowers. She laughs like a little kid chasing bubbles. I smile too—her laughter is infectious, but something twists in my gut.

It's *my* magic.

"Okay, come on," I say, and I grab her hand. I can't watch anymore. She spins me around before coming to a stop. "Let's go inside so we can find out what's going on."

Artemis greets us with her flair, leading us into the parlor before disappearing to make tea. While we wait on the couch, Ingrid fidgets. She gets up on her knees and leans over the back of the couch, reaching out to the line of plants in front of the windowsill. Her hand brushes the leaves, and they blossom in front of her, green vines spilling out from the pots.

"What are you doing!?" I grab her sleeve and try to pull her down, but she just laughs and pulls away from me.

"It's fun!"

She jumps up and dances around the room. The vines spread over the dark wooden floor. I pull my knees up to my chest so the foliage doesn't touch my feet. Ingrid throws her head back, whooping. Her hair comes loose from her ponytail and spills around her shoulders. Green tendrils crawl up her body and sit on her skin like a spider silk dress. She looks like a crazy forest fairy, not my sister.

"Stop it!"

Ingrid ignores me. That's when I notice that something is off about her. A wispy, green glow surrounds her entire body. Just like the stone, she's glowing.

I pull the stone out of my pocket. Still gray as any other river rock. I grip my legs tighter and squeeze my eyes shut. I want this all to stop. I want it all to go away.

"Oh, my."

Artemis stands in the doorway holding a tray with a pot of tea and three cups. The room has been transformed around us. Every piece of furniture—even the walls and ceiling—is draped in mossy, green growth. Only my small couch has been spared. Ingrid drops her arms. She's ruined Artemis's entire living room.

Then, something incredible happens. The green starts to recede. It slips down the walls and across the floor, back into the four small plant pots it started from, as if it were being sucked up by a vacuum. As if time were moving backward. After a few moments, the living room looks as if Ingrid's magical outburst had never happened. The only evidence is her wild hair and shining eyes.

"That was incredible!" Ingrid shouts.

Artemis steps around her to set the tea down on a low table, never taking her eyes off Ingrid.

"Yes, it was...tell me, is this the first time you've used such magic?"

"Today was the first time," she says, nodding. "And earlier, when I touched Juniper's shoulder, the magic came out of her too."

Artemis cocks her head and looks at me. I hold out my hand. The gray stone sits lifeless in my palm.

"I wanted to tell you last time," I say quietly. "My magic hasn't worked since...you know. I was hoping you could explain it."

Artemis looks contemplatively between the two of us.

"Very curious." She pours us each a cup of tea and sits down on the piano bench. "I have a theory. Juniper, you poured all your magic into bringing Ingrid back. It's very possible that, in the process, you somehow transferred all your magical ability to her."

I look over at Ingrid. She doesn't seem to be paying attention. She holds her teacup in one hand and spins a white flower between two fingers in the other.

"Is there any way to get it back?"

"Of course." Artemis sips her tea. "Either experience another magical event or put in decades of rigorous study."

"Decades! But that's not fair!"

I already poured so much of myself into learning magic to bring Ingrid back. I broke rules and lost the closest thing I had to a friend. But it was worth it to have my sister in my life again. Do I really have to give up magic now too? Especially when the one who stole it from me is the person I love most?

Artemis watches Ingrid spin the flower. It was a small flower before, its petals no bigger than a dime. But in her hands it grows and morphs into a brilliant white rose, complete with thick, sharp thorns.

"Brilliant," Artemis mutters. "Just brilliant. Wonderful control."

"I still want to do magic," I say. "I still want to study it and do experiments with you. And Ingrid."

"I won't go back on my bargain, regardless of the circumstances," Artemis says. "In fact, I've made some preparations in anticipation of your visit. Care to follow me?"

Artemis leads us into the library, heels clacking against the wooden floor, and Ingrid and I follow.

The Elm House library is something out of a dream. Floor-to-ceiling oak shelves line the walls, complete with a ladder that slides along the bookcases. A velvet wingback chair sits in front of the fireplace, with a stack of leather-bound books on a small table beside it. There's another door on the far side of the room, and Artemis stops in front of it. On the wall beside the door is a small black-and-white photo in a gold frame. It's a portrait of a girl about my age. Her hair is light and cropped in a short bob with a bow on the side, and she wears an old-fashioned dress.

"Who is that?" I ask.

Artemis purses her lips. Her dark eyes look sad while she looks at the portrait.

"This is Ruby." She says, letting out a breath.

202

I study the portrait carefully, thinking about all the notes scrawled in the margins. For some reason, I pictured Ruby being older. I imagined her to be a lot like Ingrid, I realize.

"More than fifty years ago now, Ruby was my apprentice. We were researching the magical plane. She was gifted—as you are, Juniper—and she had such a keen mind for magic. But one day…we went too far with our experiments. It was my fault. I pushed her too much. And she was lost."

"Lost how?" Ingrid asks. "Did she die?"

"No, she didn't." Artemis looks up at the ceiling. "The experiment was successful. We proved, without a doubt, that the magical plane exists."

"That's why her notes were in that book," I say. "She was helping you research the magical plane."

"She was a brilliant assistant," Artemis says.

"So what went wrong?" I ask.

"She's stuck there," Artemis says. "Her soul is trapped on the magical plane, possibly forever. That is, unless I can get her back."

This must be what Soren meant when he warned me about the people Artemis had hurt. Ruby was one of those people. But it's not like Artemis meant for her to get stuck—it was a lab accident. If we get her back, maybe Soren will realize that Artemis's experiments aren't so bad.

"How?" I ask.

"My plan was to bring her back the same way you brought Ingrid back," Artemis says. "Your powers were able to create a new body for Ingrid's soul. I believe that we can do the same thing for Ruby. Although, if your magic is gone…"

"If we did it once, we can do it again," I say, sounding more confident than I feel.

"There is more I want to show you." She grabs the handle of the other door and pushes it open. "This is the dining room. I don't use it for dining much anymore."

I haven't seen this room before. There is a white marble fireplace and a long table to seat over a dozen people. But that is where the resemblance to a dining room ends. The chairs are stacked up in the corner and covered with a dusty white sheet. The table is covered in books, papers, and scientific equipment. There's a strong smell of formaldehyde—the chemical used to preserve dead things. My heart lurches at what lies in the center of the table.

A body.

But it's not a real body at all. It's a mannequin. The limbs and skull are made of white wood, and the joints are smooth but lined with seams. There are pencil markings all over the figure— some of them are chemical equations, but others are circles and scribblings in another language. The entire thing is covered in a thick layer of dust.

"Years ago, I experimented on dummies, trying to find a way to bring Ruby back. I tried everything, but no matter what I did, I couldn't meld body and soul. Not until I met you, and your magic brought back Ingrid."

She steps around the table and runs a finger along the dummy's skull.

"I like to think of it this way. The body is science—with the right materials and equations I can put the body together like building an engine. The body is the machine that carries us around. Your magic created Ingrid's body easily. But what makes us really who we are? That's the soul. It's ephemeral. It's magic. Only under very specific, very difficult circumstances can we put body and soul together."

I look at the carved wooden head. It's egg-shaped, with no facial features. Just a smooth white surface. It doesn't look anything like a real person.

"But what about her soul?" I glance at Ingrid. "How did I get it before?"

Artemis looks at me a long time before answering.

"Some things in magic are ineffable, indescribable," Artemis says cryptically. "But I know with absolute certainty that Ruby's soul resides on the magical plane. My objective is this: make the body, find the soul, and put them together."

I look at Ingrid. She is glancing all around the room. It's hard for me to tell what she is thinking. Once upon a time, I could look at her and know exactly how she felt. Everything she did, she did for science, for facts, for knowledge. But now, I'm not so sure. Helping Artemis with this new experiment might be the only way to figure Ingrid out.

"We're in."

Chapter 17

Artemis leads us back into the room with the piano. The tea has gone cold—she taps a gold-ringed finger against the cups, and steam rises off the liquid once again.

"Now that we're all on the same page, I think it's time to begin your magical education, Ingrid." Artemis takes a long sip of her tea. "Of course, I require a promise from you: that you will keep everything you learn about magic in the utmost secrecy."

"I will," Ingrid promises. "How do I start?"

"I think it might be wise to start in the same way I had Juniper start. A classic literature review."

"Reading?" Ingrid asks. "I already have a lot of homework."

"I guarantee this will be more interesting than *The Great Gatsby*," Artemis says, then turns to me. "Juniper, my first task for you as my new lab assistant: I have a second copy of *Alchymy, Magicks, and Natural Philosophy* in my laboratory. Could you fetch it for us? I'd like to have a moment alone with Ingrid."

Something hot burns in my chest. There's nothing Artemis can say to Ingrid that she can't say to me. I leave the room without a word. I wanted to help with the research, not run errands. Is this all I'm good for, now that Ingrid has my magic?

The floorboards creak under my footsteps as I enter Artemis's laboratory on the second floor. The room is still littered with books and papers, but many of them look newly disheveled. I see a lot of hastily scratched equations and diagrams. Artemis has already been working on this new project. The featureless face of the mannequin downstairs flashes before my eyes, and I shiver. There is something about it that creeps me out. But this is the best chance I have for reconnecting with Ingrid. It's a secret she and I will share—she can't tell our parents or her new friends. It'll be just the two of us, besides Artemis and Soren.

I find the familiar magic book on a shelf and pull it down. I can't help flipping it open. It's missing Ruby's annotations. At least that's something I'll have that Ingrid doesn't.

I close the book and turn toward the door, but something moves in the corner of my vision. I freeze, and I glance toward the couch.

"Soren?"

A head pops out from behind the couch, but it's not Soren's. It's the head of a boy with a mop of brown, frizzy hair.

"Mateo!" I whisper-shout his name, not wanting anyone to hear, then briskly close the door to the hallway before anyone notices. "What are you doing here?"

Mateo stands up. His clothes are grass-stained and dirty.

"I followed you."

"I thought you hated me," I say.

"I saw what you did to Chelsea," he said. "And what your sister did. When I saw you crawl through the bushes to this house, I had to see what was here."

"You shouldn't have come here."

"You lied to me," he says. "You lied to me about magic, *and* you lied about this house. What else did you lie about?"

Footsteps in the hallway stop me from answering. Mateo and I both look at the door, eyes wide. I motion for Mateo to hide, and he ducks back down behind the couch just as the door opens.

"And this is my laboratory, where I do most of my work." Artemis and Ingrid step inside the room. "Oh, Juniper! You found it."

It takes me a second to remember the book I have tucked under my arm.

"Yep. Here it is." I hand Artemis the book, hoping she doesn't notice my shaking voice. I promised I would keep magic a secret.

"This will give you the fundamentals," Artemis says, handing the book to Ingrid. "Study it carefully, just as your sister did. Then we can begin to test the true strength of your powers."

Ingrid takes the book and looks at it skeptically.

"Come," Artemis says. "There's more to show—are you coming, Juniper?"

"Um, I'll be right down," I say, and grab a random book off the desk. "Is it okay if I take a look at this for a bit?"

Artemis cocks an eyebrow. "I had no idea you had an interest in corvid numerology."

"It just looks so interesting." I give what I hope is a convincing smile.

Artemis shrugs. "Of course. I found it to be dull hogwash myself. But go on. Now Ingrid, as I was saying…"

She leads Ingrid out of the room, and their footsteps disappear down the stairs.

Mateo pops his head out from behind the couch again.

"Is it safe?" he asks.

I throw the book back onto the desk.

"You need to get out of here. Right. Now."

"No way," he says. "I just got here. I want to explore. If there are other magicians in the neighborhood, it's only fair that I know about it."

"The magicians in this house are old and powerful. If they catch you, I don't know what they'll do, but I know I'll be in trouble."

"Fine," Mateo says, crossing his arms. "But you can't lie to me anymore."

"I didn't want to lie to you," I say. "I was sworn to secrecy. Can we talk about this later? We need to leave."

Mateo frowns, but gestures for me to lead. I peek out the door to make sure the coast is clear. No one in the hallway. I beckon for Mateo to follow. We walk lightly toward the stairs, careful not to let the floorboards squeak under our feet. At the top of the stairs we hear voices from down below.

"We can't go this way," I whisper. I look around, panicking, and remember my mom's period dramas. Old houses like these always have separate stairs for servants. I wonder if the Elm House does too. I spin around and dash back down the hall until we reach the final door, hoping it's not a bathroom. I push the door open, revealing a narrow staircase.

"Come on," I say, closing the door behind us. We make our way down the steps, and I hope these lead us to the kitchen so that we can sneak out the back door.

When we reach the bottom, my hand is on the door handle when I hear a voice.

"I don't have much time for cooking anymore, but certain magical enhancements make it easier. Would you like a scone?"

I turn around and practically push Mateo back up the stairs. If Artemis is in the kitchen, we'll have to find another way out. We go up past the second floor and keep climbing.

The stairs end at a square door set in the ceiling. The handle is a metal loop. I yank on it, but the door doesn't budge. Set in the handle is a keyhole.

"A dead end!" I groan.

"Wait," Mateo says. He lifts his hand to his mouth, then

gives me an apologetic look. "Sorry about this."

Mateo spits into his hand and rubs the saliva on the lock. He closes his eyes, and something glows from beneath his shirt. His necklace. The keyhole frosts over with ice, and there's a loud crack.

Mateo pulls on the handle again, and this time the door swings open. A great gust of dust blows out on us, and my eyes water.

Mateo and I stand on our tiptoes to peer into the hole. It's hard to see from the dust and the darkness.

"I think it's an attic," Mateo says.

"Go in," I whisper to him. "Hide, and I'll come get you when the coast is clear."

Mateo climbs up, headfirst, but stops halfway in.

"Um, Juniper?" Mateo's voice is a hoarse whisper.

"What?"

"You have to see this."

He climbs the rest of the way in, and I follow. I cover my mouth so I don't breathe in the thick, ancient dust that fills the air. The deeply slanted ceiling is only about three feet high, so I can't stand up all the way. I pull the trap door closed behind us. It's dark in the attic. There's a small rectangular window on the opposite end, but it only lets in a very small amount of light.

"What is all this?" Mateo asks. His voice sounds small—and terrified.

At first, I thought the room was filled with clutter, like attics often are. But then I realize the shapes littered around the attic aren't regular piles of junk.

They're bodies.

More specifically, they're mannequins. Dolls. Bent and disfigured in inhuman ways. Some of them are missing limbs, some of them are burnt beyond recognition. They're like the dummy I saw on the dining room table, but worse. Failures. And they're all covered in a thick layer of dust.

"What…what's going on in this house?" Mateo's voice shakes.

I swallow and look away from the uncanny corpses. I knew that Artemis had tried this experiment before. Soren had told me about her failures. But I didn't know there were this many.

"Science. I think." I trusted Artemis because she took me seriously as a scientist. But now, I'm not so sure.

There's a gentle tap on the trap door. Mateo jumps and spins around, lifting his arms defensively. But I hear a familiar voice.

"It's okay, Juniper," Soren says, opening the door a crack. "I'll help your friend leave undetected."

The sound of Soren's voice makes me relax. I push the door back open, and there's Soren, standing on his lemur legs. Mateo stiffens beside me.

"I've seen you before," he says. "Are you a monkey?"

"Lemur," Soren says. "Sadly, there's no time for introductions. I'm going to create a diversion. Go down through the kitchen and out the front door. Mateo will go out through the passage—and Juniper, come up with an excuse for why you're in the garden."

Soren scampers down the stairs. Mateo and I clamber out of

the attic, and I'm glad to be away from the creepy mannequins.

When we get to the bottom of the stairs, the kitchen is empty. Mateo follows me through the door that leads to the main hall, and we both burst out the heavy wooden doors and into the sunshine.

"You owe me an explanation," Mateo says as we sprint across the grass. "For everything."

He gets down on his hands and knees and crawls through the opening in the fence, just as Soren, Ingrid, and Artemis emerge from around the side of the house.

"See?" Soren says. "I knew I saw her in the garden."

"We were looking for you!" Ingrid says, running up to me. A trail of brilliant blue flowers springs up behind her. I forgot to make up an excuse.

"I was, uh…" I look down at the grass under my feet. "Trying to see if my power is back?"

I bend down and lay my palms against the grass to demonstrate. The grass wavers in the wind, but nothing grows.

"My dear," Artemis says with a sigh. "I'm afraid it seems that the magic has left you for now. But through hard work, you can get it back."

I look down at my feet. I hate the sound in her voice—it's the same tone my parents and teachers would use whenever Ingrid was mentioned after she died. Pity.

A ding comes from Ingrid's pocket. She pulls out her new phone and starts typing.

"I need to go," she says, without looking up. "I promised Lucy I'd get Froyo with her."

"But you promised you'd come here and do science with me," I say.

"And I did, see?" Ingrid says, holding up the book. "Even got extra homework out of it."

She tucks the book under her arm and starts to crawl through the fence. She grows a bed of green clovers grow beneath her so the mud doesn't get on her clothes.

"I'm afraid I've been neglecting some of my other duties," Artemis says, producing gloves out of nowhere and pulling them over her fingers. "I promised a friend down in Irvine I'd help with a spiritual matter, and if I don't leave soon traffic will be unbearable. Until next time, Juniper."

Artemis disappears into the house, leaving me and Soren alone in the garden.

"It isn't fair," I say.

He blinks. "What isn't?"

"Everything." I kick at some of the small vines Ingrid grew, tearing them from the soil. Soren jumps onto my back and perches himself on my shoulder. He's surprisingly light. He leans close to my ear.

"Are you mad that Ingrid has magic now, and you don't?"

"A little," I admit. "But I wouldn't care so much if she was more interested in research. Instead of studying magic, she's getting Froyo. And what about the Blue? It was her whole life, and she acts like it doesn't matter anymore. I just…I feel like she isn't the same person she used to be."

Soren climbs around my neck to my other shoulder, his fur brushing gently against the back of my head.

"I imagine death would change a person," he says.

"I suppose you're right," I say. Ingrid hasn't talked about what it was like to be dead. I've been too afraid to ask.

"People change, Juniper, and so do their interests. Your relationship with your sister might not be what it was…but perhaps this is an opportunity to form a new, stronger bond."

"But I don't want anything to change," I say. "I want everything to be the way it was."

"Even someone like Artemis has changed over the years, and certainly I have. The way we are with each other might be different, and sure, we have our disagreements, yet for over a hundred years, neither of us has ever thought about living a life without the other. Love is like milk."

"Milk?"

"It never truly goes bad. It only changes form."

"No, milk definitely goes bad."

"You just aren't being imaginative." Soren jumps down and brushes off his fur. "Well, forget it. You'd best be off doing whatever it is you do, and I'll be off doing whatever it is I do."

He turns and disappears behind the hedges.

Bringing Ingrid here was supposed to make her forget about her new friends so she'd do research with me again. But it didn't

215

work. Mateo hates me, my sister abandoned me, my magic is gone, and I don't know if there's even a place for me in Artemis's new experiment. As I crawl through the gap in the fence between the Elm House and my house, I feel more alone than ever.

PART VI

Repeat

Chapter 18

That night, I see flashes of the dusty, blank-faced mannequins every time I doze off, and it jolts me awake. I barely get any sleep, and the next morning, I get ready in a groggy haze.

When I finally stumble out the front door, Ingrid and Dad are waiting in the car. Ingrid is in the front, tapping on her new phone. My eyes feel heavy.

"Will you be here after school?" I ask Ingrid as the car pulls up to the drop-off line.

"Uh-huh," Ingrid says, not looking up from her phone.

I will try to talk to Mateo during English. We can't say much in the middle of class, but maybe I can ask if he wants to talk at lunch. That will be a good start. I spend all of my first period math class thinking about what I'm going to say. Sorry I lied about the magic house next door and then did a dangerous experiment that used up all my magic, even though you told me not to?

Five minutes before the end of math class, the classroom phone rings. Ms. Nguyen, the math teacher, glares at the phone before answering it. When she hangs it up, her eyes flick to me.

"Juniper, they want you in the office."

The entire class says, "Ooooooh!"

I shrink down in my chair, their eyes burning into mine as I slide my things into my backpack. Why am I wanted in the office? Could it be because of what happened with Chelsea yesterday?

"The rest of you, don't pack up yet!" Ms. Nguyen wields her whiteboard marker like a sword. "We still have five minutes."

When I get to the office, the secretary smiles up at me.

"Juniper, right?" I nod, and she sticks a thumb over her shoulder. "They're waiting for you in Mrs. Barrett's office."

I gulp. Mrs. Barrett is a nice principal. She's always walking through the halls, complimenting people's outfits and making an effort to remember names. When we raised a bunch of money during the last school fundraiser, she dyed her hair pink for a week. But if I'm being sent to her office, it means I'm in trouble.

The door to the principal's office is already open. And I find out who the "they" are—it's my parents and Mrs. Cartwright, along with Mrs. Barrett.

My parents smile at me. Mrs. Cartwright doesn't. Mrs. Barrett is dressed more like a fancy TV lawyer than a principal. She has really high heels and a pencil skirt, and her hair falls in perfect curls on either side of her head. She stands up and beams a smile bright enough to be on a dentist commercial, rimmed with perfect pink lipstick.

"Juniper!" She talks as if we are best friends. I don't think she's ever talked to me before. "Thanks for coming in."

It's not like I was given a choice. I nod and take the last remaining chair. My hands shake.

"Now, there's no reason to be nervous," she says. "We are just going to have a conversation."

Mrs. Cartwright hands Mrs. Barrett a rolled-up poster, and I know exactly what it is. She unrolls it onto her desk. She uses a stapler and little potted cactus to hold down the corners. Mom and Dad lean forward to peer at it.

"Looks like good work," Dad mumbles.

"It is good work," Mrs. Cartwright says. "Juniper is a very bright student who is clearly passionate about science. But that's not the problem here."

My science teacher leans forward and pulls at the corner of one of the pages of text. It lifts up, and underneath it one of Chelsea's drawings becomes visible. It's an owl with cartoonishly large eyes.

"This was a group project. While the project was initially rather impressive, the other student came to me with some concerns that her portion had been disrespected. Here's the grade sheet—you'll see that they lost points for creativity. The other student believes they would've gotten a higher grade if Juniper hadn't changed the project. The word she used was 'sabotage.'"

Dad takes the grade sheet.

"'Sabotage' seems a little excessive," Mom says. "I'm sure Juniper didn't do this out of malice."

"Can you tell us what happened, Juniper?" Principal Barrett says.

"I…I just wanted to get a good grade. So I changed some things."

Dad puts the paper on the desk.

"Look, I'm a professor. I deal with group projects all the time. If a student is turning something in with their name on it, that's like their seal of approval. It's on them to look it over and make sure they know what they're turning in. I find it hard to believe that this is solely Juniper's fault—I mean, look at all the work that was done! This other partner must not have looked at the project at all if Juniper managed to write all this on top of it. The other girl should be at fault too. Not to mention, this hardly seems like something worth calling us in for."

"Maybe not," Mrs. Cartwright says slowly. "And if this were an isolated incident, then I'd likely handle it in the classroom. But there have been consistent…issues with Juniper's behavior. The same sort of issues I had with Ingrid when she was in my class. They let passion get in the way of schoolwork. The incident at the nature preserve is a perfect example—leaving the group, going off trail—"

"But that was an accident," Mom says.

Mrs. Barrett and Mrs. Cartwright look at each other.

"It happened after Juniper deliberately broke the rules," Mrs. Barrett says. Her voice has gone from sweet to stern. "And there is also what happened after that, when Juniper left school in the middle of the day."

I sink lower into my chair, waiting for Mrs. Barrett to tell my parents about how I attacked Chelsea with plants. Scary words race through my brain: Assault. Expulsion. Disappointment.

"Juniper is a bright student, but this is all very concerning behavior," Mrs. Barrett says to my parents. I relax a little as I realize she might not know about the attack. Maybe Chelsea didn't tell.

Mrs. Barrett waits for my parents to answer with her hands folded neatly on the desk in front of her. This is the part where my parents pull out the sob story—I'm just going through so much since Ingrid died, and they'll put me in therapy again, yada yada.

But they don't. Ingrid's not dead to them anymore, so I don't have any excuses. Instead they both turn and frown at me. They look concerned. Disappointed.

Impossibly, I sink lower.

"What's going on, June?" Dad's voice is quiet and gentle. Friendly, even. Somehow that makes it worse. I'd rather they be angry and yell at me. But they don't.

"We just want Juniper to succeed," Mrs. Barrett says. "Instead of disciplinary action, we're willing to put together a plan—one that we can all agree on—to help Juniper get back on the right track."

For the rest of the meeting, the adults make decisions about me that I get no say in. I feel lower than dirt as my parents discuss things like weekly meetings with the school counselor. At the end, we all have to sign their plan for me. Mrs. Barrett looks at me.

"One last thing," she says. "I want you to find a way to apologize to Chelsea."

"I will," I say.

"Do you mean it, though?" She tilts her head to the side. She waits a moment, then smiles. "It's not a question I can answer for you. Figure out a way apologize meaningfully, and then report back to me. You're a smart girl. I'm sure you can think of something."

I look for Mateo at lunch, but I don't see him, so I sit at the wobbly table all by myself again. I do my best to avoid Chelsea and her group's mean stares.

I still don't think it's fair that I'm the one who got in trouble. Maybe our creativity grade could've been better, but I'm the one who did most of the work. If I hadn't written the actual science sections, our grade would've been even lower.

I look for Ingrid after school, but she isn't waiting for me at the edge of the sidewalk. I sit down on the low wall next to the school's steps and wait. I pull out the new notebook we've been working on together—well, the one I've been working on. Ingrid hasn't contributed much of anything to it.

I spent two years of my life obsessed with finding the Palos Verdes Blue. I told myself I was doing it for her. Now, I'm not so sure.

"I won't ask if that's a diary." Mateo hops onto the ledge next to me. "More field research?"

I snap the notebook shut. "I wish."

"Are you waiting for your sister?"

I look around. The front of the school is clear of cars. There are a few kids waiting for their parents by the parking lot, but everyone else is gone. It's just me and Mateo.

"I don't think she's coming, actually."

"We could walk home together. If you want."

It's not forgiveness, but it's something. We hope off the wall and start to walk. There are so many things I want to say, but I don't know how to begin. Mateo is quiet too. I wonder if he's feeling the same way.

When we get to our street, Mateo stops in front of the Elm House. We peer through the front gate.

"Has it always looked this way to you?" I ask him.

"What do you mean?"

"When I fell in the creek on our field trip—that's when I got magic." I shiver as I remember the feeling of the cold water dragging me under. "Before that, this house looked boarded up. All the windows were broken, and the garden was overgrown. But after I fell, everything changed."

"It looks the same as it always has to me," he says. "We have a ton of old Victorian houses where I'm from, so I didn't think anything was weird about it. Not until you tried to convince me it was abandoned."

"I'm subtle, aren't I?"

Mateo smirks.

"You might as well have put a big sign on the fence that says 'magical mystery.'"

"Well, mystery solved," I say.

"Not quite," Mateo says. "Come on, let's talk at my house."

Mateo's aunt isn't home when we get there. We go straight up to his room. The carpet is completely clean—I wonder how hard it was to get all the dead leaf bits out, and I feel a pang of guilt for leaving such a mess for Mateo and Tía Barbara. I sit down on the floor and Mateo sits across from me.

"I'm not going to apologize for not telling you about the house." My voice is a low, breathy whisper, as if talking too loudly will break our fragile safety. "Artemis made me swear not tell anyone."

"I can understand that." He lifts a hand and runs it through his shaggy curls. "I don't exactly go around sharing my secrets, either. But now I know, and I don't think there's any reason to keep any more secrets from each other. 'Truth will out' and all that."

I give him a confused look and his cheeks turn red.

"Sorry. It's from Shakespeare," he says. "Tell me how you met Artemis."

I start at the beginning: falling in the creek and finding the stone, Soren coming to my window, the incident in English class, Artemis giving me the book.

"I asked you to help me because I wanted to impress her," I explain. "She said if I learned to control my power, she'd let me be her assistant."

"And did she?"

"Well, sort of. But it's not the same if I can't do magic," I say. "How come Soren and Artemis never found you?"

"My aunt has wards on the house," Mateo says. "My parents insisted. They didn't want to leave me unprotected, and experienced magic users are pretty good at sniffing out other magicians."

"That must be how they found me," I say. "Artemis has the same thing on the Elm House, so that nonmagical people can't see it. She called it a glamour."

"Same kind of spell," Mateo says. "It changes how people see things."

"Maybe I can introduce you to them," I say. "Officially. Then we can study magic together."

"No way," Mateo says. "My parents would be so mad if they

found out. I'm not supposed to use magic at all. But it's part of me. It'll never really be gone."

I look down at my hands. There was a time, not too long ago, when I wanted nothing to do with magic. But now that I've had it and lost it, I want it back more than anything. It's more than just something I can study—like Mateo said, it was part of me. And now it's gone.

"There's something else I have to tell you." Mateo's voice has gone quieter, and his cheeks are red. "That day at the nature preserve, when you went off the path and fell...I followed you."

"You did?" I wrack my brain, but I don't remember seeing him.

"I'd been trying to listen to my parents and not use my magic, but when I saw you fall..." He holds out his hands, palms up, and looks at them. "Water's my specialty. I couldn't do nothing. So I used my power to get you out."

"*You* saved me?" I remember how icy the water had felt, even on a warm day, and it all makes sense.

"I called for help right after, but I was worried that if I waited it would be too late."

I stare at Mateo. All this time I thought he was the weird new kid, but now he is the weird new kid who saved my life. And he's also pretty cool.

"Wow. Well. Thanks."

"You helped me get out of the Elm House, so I guess it's even."

"It was stupid to come in the first place when I specifically told you not to."

"You're one to talk about following the rules," Mateo says. "If you were on the brink of a scientific discovery and someone told you to stop, would you?"

"No, I guess I wouldn't."

"Well, it's the same for me. Except for me, it's all about the story."

For so long I thought Mateo was like an alien—that's how different we were. Now I see that even though we like different things, we have a lot of similarities.

"Please don't hate me for saying this, Juniper, but Artemis seems dangerous," he says. "What's with all those creepy mannequins? My parents study magic too, but I've never seen anything like that."

"She's trying to bring another girl back," I say. "Her name is Ruby. I'm supposed to help. Well...I was going to. My magic doesn't work anymore. And Ingrid's back, but she's all wrong. I wanted to fix everything, but I feel like I just made everything worse."

"Some things you can't fix," Mateo says. "Not even with magic."

"Then how can I make it better? Am I supposed to just be miserable?"

"I have a few ideas," Mateo says. "But they're not very scientific. Do you want to try something new?"

"Trying new things is the heart of science," I correct.

Mateo goes to his desk and pulls out a notebook and a pen.

"No way," I groan. "Not poetry."

He thrusts the notebook and pen into my hands.

"Maybe the one thing you hate is the thing you need the most."

I do something I thought I would never do: I write a poem. Well, Mateo helps. He also reads me poetry to help me find inspiration. And I actually listen. It's kind of nice. He reads from a book by Robert Frost. A lot of the poems are about nature, and observations of plants and animals, which I like. Mateo insists there's a deeper, more metaphorical meaning. I'm not so sure, but we agree to disagree.

It takes two hours, several sheets of notebook paper, a few heated arguments over the dictionary, and a lot crossing out and rearranging, but I finally have a poem. Not just one for class, but one—I realize—for me. As much as I hate to admit it, I do feel a little better.

I don't realize how late it is until Tía Barbara gets home.

"Ah, Juniper! What a surprise!" We come down the stairs as she is taking off her shoes. "Would you like to stay for dinner?"

"I'd better get home, but thank you." I turn to Mateo. "Next time, you should come to my house. I'll show you bugs."

"Deal." He seems a lot more excited about bugs than I did about poetry. That's understandable, since insects are objectively better.

Mom and Dad get home right after I do. Dad makes spaghetti

and meatballs for dinner. I hum to myself as I pour a glass of milk.

"Are you…humming?" Dad looks over his shoulder at me from the stove.

"Um. I didn't mean to."

"No, don't stop," Dad says. He turns back to the pot on the stove. "I'm just surprised. I don't think I've ever heard you hum. You're in good spirits considering what happened today."

Oh. Right. The principal's office. I'd honestly forgotten until he said something. Hanging out at Mateo's house was like pressing the reset button on my brain. I sit down at the table next to Mom.

"Have you thought about what Mrs. Barrett said?" Dad asks as he drains the pasta.

"Which part?"

"The apologizing part."

I take a long drink of milk before answering him.

"I don't see why just saying 'sorry' isn't enough."

Dad sighs. "I can tell by your tone of voice that you're not sorry."

"Why should I be?" I counter, my good mood evaporating. "All I wanted was to get a good grade. Why should I apologize to someone who didn't do even half the work that I did? Why should she get the apology and not me?"

Mom and Dad exchange a concerned glance, just like the ones they have when we talk about Ingrid. Or used to, before she came back. Where is Ingrid anyway? Probably off with her new high school friends.

Dad sets plates of spaghetti and meatballs in front of us. Mine is covered in parmesan, just the way I like it, but I don't really feel hungry anymore. He scoots his chair close to mine.

"Do you know what the most important part of being a scientist is?" he asks.

"Stay curious. Study hard. Record accurate data. Follow the scientific method—" I rattle off all the wise sayings Dad has repeated over the years. But he stops me, shaking his head.

"No," he says. "None of that. These days, everyone wants to go into science or engineering. But here's the thing—your success doesn't depend on how well you can do math or write programs. What matters is how you communicate. The scientists who can explain their findings well will go farther than those who can't write papers to save their lives. In science, you're always working together, building off each other's research, taking part in a global conversation. You're not just one person going out into the world and making great discoveries on your own. You're part of the world, like everyone else, and you need to learn how to work with that world even if you'd rather not."

"But Chelsea doesn't want to be a scientist," I retort. "She wants to be an artist."

"And she knows her strengths. It seems to me like she tried to give you a chance to show yours, but you trampled on hers instead."

I think about Mateo, and how I thought poetry was stupid

until I gave it an honest chance. Maybe I was unfair to Chelsea about this project. I let my desire to be a scientist get in the way of being a nice person. I push my plate away from me.

"I'm not hungry anymore," I say. An idea dawns on me. "But I think I know how I'm going to apologize."

I run up the stairs and tip over the small wastebasket by my desk. Crumped papers and a few empty chip bags spill out. At the bottom are the photos and sketches I'd torn off the poster board. I pull them out and try my best to flatten them.

I have a lot of work to do.

Chapter 19

The next day, I assume Ingrid won't be there to pick me up, so Mateo and I make plans to walk home together. But as we walk down the steps of the school, a figure across the street catches my eye. Artemis stands on the other side of the road, wearing wide-legged trousers and a white button-down shirt. She looks completely out of place with round sunglasses and a black lace umbrella shielding her from the sun. I freeze when I see her. I've never seen her outside the Elm House before. It's jarring to see her surrounded by bustling middle schoolers with backpacks. They don't seem to notice her—everyone floods past, not sparing her a second glance.

"Why is she here?" Mateo asks.

"Don't know," I say. I start to move toward her, but Mateo

catches my wrist.

"She's dangerous," he says.

I pull my wrist back. "I'll be fine."

I give him an apologetic smile before jogging down the steps and crossing the street.

"Juniper! Just the girl I came to see," she says, grinning. "Learn anything interesting today?"

"Not really," I say.

"Ah, well. I suppose that's to be expected of American school." Artemis turns to walk down the street, and I fall into step beside her.

"What are you doing here?" I ask.

"I do like to step out occasionally, you know," she says, twirling her umbrella over her shoulder. "All this California sunshine is wasted on me. I miss the London fog."

"So you just happened to be out for a walk?" I ask skeptically. I look over my shoulder back at Mateo. He's following us, blending in with the crowd of kids rushing to get out of school.

"Only because I wanted to speak with you," Artemis replies.

We continue past the park and into the quiet neighborhood. Artemis walks slowly, as if she's out for a leisurely afternoon stroll, and it's almost agonizing to keep her pace. Once we are away from anyone else, she speaks again.

"What do you think of Ingrid?" she asks.

The question catches me off guard.

"It's nice to have her back," I say truthfully. "But…"

Artemis turns and cocks an eyebrow at me over the round lenses of her sunglasses. "But?"

"She's—not how I remember," I say, chewing my lip. "She's different."

"People change as they grow older," Artemis says. "Or perhaps death changes them."

"Maybe," I say.

"Or perhaps—ah! Look!" She stops abruptly in front of a small house. The yard is enclosed by a white fence, and behind it is an overgrown tangle of plants. But it's springtime, and the plants are blooming, flowers sprouting wildly on trellises and across the ground. "A lovely bit of chaos, isn't it?"

"Perhaps what?" I prompt, tugging on Artemis's sleeve.

Artemis runs her fingers along some of the leaves that are sticking out through the boards of the fence.

"I've spent some time with Ingrid, as you know," she says.

Jealousy pangs my stomach. Of course. Ingrid is the new magical prodigy now, not me.

"I've been observing her," she continues. "Analyzing her. I don't know what your sister used to be like as well as you do, but from what I can tell, she's very different."

Observing? Is that all Artemis was doing? Getting Ingrid alone so that she could observe her? Maybe Artemis wasn't trying to get rid of me, but just wanted to analyze Ingrid. I feel simultaneously relieved and foolish.

"There's some similarities," I say. "But...it's like she's a different person."

Artemis hums, refocusing on the sidewalk as we continue on our slow walk toward our street. We turn another corner, and the iron fence of the Elm House comes into view.

"I do not want to be indelicate, because I know how much she means to you, but we are scientists. I think it best to be straightforward." She removes her sunglasses and turns her brown eyes on me. "Juniper, do you feel certain that the individual you created in the nature preserve is your sister?"

Hearing Artemis say those words out loud, in broad daylight, in the middle of the street, sends a shiver of unease through me. Magic is hidden in old houses and secret notebooks. It feels wrong for Artemis to even be outside at all, but at the same time, it makes everything feel more real. It also feels more impossible. Could I really have brought a person back from the dead, with just a few short days of magical training?

I want to believe it. I want to believe that Ingrid is really here and that everything is the way it was before she died. But I hesitate. Ingrid is so different than I remember. Maybe...

No. The thought makes my chest ache.

"She has to be," I insist. "Who else could she be?"

"You know your sister better than I do," Artemis says. "But I'm asking you not to think like sister, but like a scientist. Based on all the evidence that you have, can you say for certain that she is the same person?"

At that moment, a car passes us, slowing to a crawl. Loud

music thumps, the deep bass reverberating in my shoes. The car stops in front of my house, and I see six heads crammed into it through the rear windshield. Laughter bubbles from the open windows. The back door opens, and Ingrid pops out. She leans through the window to show someone in the backseat something on her phone. My eyes linger on her, but she doesn't even notice me.

Ingrid loved reading field guides and getting dirty. This new person likes nice clothes and makeup and body spray. There's nothing wrong with that, but it's not what Ingrid was like. It's not what we were like.

Maybe Artemis is right. Maybe this person is not Ingrid. I watch her laugh with her friends, her blond hair shining in the sunlight. She looks exactly like my sister. But the real Ingrid never would have abandoned science the way this person has. She would never have abandoned me.

"But...if she isn't Ingrid, then who is she?"

"For my part, I do not think she is anyone," Artemis explains. "I have a new theory. You didn't bring Ingrid back. You created the body, but you lacked the most important part: the soul. Instead you created a new Ingrid, one based on memory. Memory, however, is fickle. Once she was her own being, she was out of your control. And you didn't give her your magic. She *is* your magic."

I feel the stone, cold and hard and lifeless in my pocket. I watch Ingrid, who has one hand on her backpack strap and the other holding her phone as she laughs. It's not fair that she has my magic when she doesn't even want it. It's not fair that I worked this hard, and she's not even my sister. I clench my fists.

"Then I failed," I say. "The experiment was a failure."

"Not failed," Artemis says. "On the contrary, considering what we've learned from that venture, I'd call it resounding success."

"We can try again," I say. "Maybe the book—"

"Juniper, I do not think there was any flaw in the execution of our experiment," she interrupts. "I think the problem was in the very premise of it—Ingrid's soul is gone. Creating a body that looks like hers was not enough to bring her back."

"But—"

"I know that this is hard for you to hear," she says. "But such is the life of a scientist—we conduct experiments, and they don't always give us the results we hope for."

"Science is meant for testing," I say, finding my voice. "We can try again. We have to. I can't live with someone walking around with my sister's face and voice, living in my house with her name and her memories. Not when I know it's not really her."

Artemis looks thoughtful.

"We can do another experiment," Artemis says slowly, watching Ingrid. "If we are lacking a soul, I know where to find one. I've been trying for years to retrieve Ruby from the magical plane. Perhaps if we put her soul in Ingrid's body…we may gather enough data to help us with future experiments."

"I'll do anything," I say. I don't have magic anymore, but I'm

241

willing to do any experiment. This one might not have worked, but maybe the next one, or the next. There must be a way to find the real Ingrid. There has to be.

Artemis gives me a sad smile. "We walk a delicate balance when we practice magic and science," she says. "Magic is all about desire—but science, it requires objectivity. Your passion burns brightly, Juniper, but you must try to be more objective."

Ingrid's friends let out one last explosion of laughter before the car finally shifts gears and zooms down the road in an eruption of music and exhaust. Not-Ingrid lingers on the sidewalk, typing out a message on her phone. It's hard to look at her objectively, to see her as Not-Ingrid. It's like I have to shift my eyes out of focus. But I know that if I want to keep doing experiments with Artemis, I need to try.

"We agree, then, that this is not your sister?" Artemis asks.

My throat seizes up, but as I watch her smile down into her phone, there is no doubt in my mind.

"We agree," I say.

Ingrid looks up, then, and spots us. She waves and walks over, breathless and smiling.

"Hey, June," she says, bumping my shoulder with hers. "What's going on?"

Artemis speaks before I can.

"Ingrid," she says, a glint of mischief in her eyes. "Care to join us for an experiment?"

242

Sunsets over the ocean are not something I usually pay much attention to. Living near the coast means that they're an everyday occurrence. I can't help but notice it today. I stand beside Ingrid in the nature preserve as Artemis draws a magic circle onto the dirt. The water looks as though it's on fire as the sun inches closer to the horizon. When I look at Ingrid, I can see the sunlight reflected in her eyes.

I can't believe that after all this time, she isn't real. She looks like Ingrid. She has the same blond hair and pointed nose. The same blue eyes and mouth that has the most wonderful smile in the world. She takes her phone out to snap a photo, but her arm goes slack, her eyes wide with wonder. A sharp breeze blows a few strands hair in front of her face, but she doesn't notice.

"Every time I think I have the world figured out, something surprises me," Ingrid says.

"What do you mean?"

She holds her palms in front of her and stares down at them.

"I can do literal magic," she says. "But it's nothing compared to this. The way the sun makes the sky pink. I know that magic is supposed to be this amazing thing, but these ordinary things that everyone experiences, like sunsets, make me feel all warm inside."

"Doesn't the magic feel good?" I ask.

Ingrid shrugs, letting her hands drop to her sides.

"It's a little lonely," she says. "But a sunset? Everyone sees it.

It makes me feel…connected somehow. Like there are thousands of people I don't know seeing this same sunset. It's like I'm a part of something, you know?"

She looks at me, but I keep my eyes ahead, over the ocean, watching it lap against the cliffs. I can't meet her eyes, not when I know what I'm about to do.

She's not real, I tell myself. She's not Ingrid.

And it must be true, because Ingrid would never get all philosophical about the sunset like that. Whatever this thing is that I created, it isn't my sister. It's like an echo of her, distorted by time and distance from the original. A photocopy.

She's not real.

Ingrid shields her eyes with her hand and turns to look south. The ships in the port are dark silhouettes against the water. Soon, glittering lights will erupt across the city, illuminating the streets and buildings. But for now, they're all cast in a golden glow.

"We should go to the beach," she says suddenly.

"What?"

"I haven't been since I've been back," she says. "I don't remember, but I think it would be nice. I want to know what the water feels like. Is it cold?"

"It can be," I say.

"Is there a good beach close to here?" she asks. "Could we take our bikes?"

"Divers discovered a bunch of toxic barrels under the water near here," I tell her. "But Dad could probably drive us…"

I trail off. There will be no driving to the beach, because after tonight, there will be no Ingrid. My throat closes up.

She's not real.

"Maybe Sunday," she says. "I'll ask—"

"I hate the beach," I blurt out. "It's too hot and there's too much sun and the sand gets everywhere and there are too many people."

Ingrid gapes at me, looking as if I just hit her. Guilt pools in the bottom of my stomach. She was so happy, and I crushed it, like crushing an insect under my heel. But I couldn't stand hearing her make plans—plans I know will never happen. I turn around and stalk back to Artemis.

"It's ready," Artemis says as I approach, standing back and admiring her handiwork.

This circle is much bigger than the one we used to bring Ingrid back. Small symbols line the inner edge of the circle, and several lines intersect in the middle. Ingrid comes and stands beside me, stiffer than before.

"What is it?" she asks.

"A door," Artemis says. She looks up to the darkening blue sky. "Do you feel it? The magic is thick here."

I look around, but I don't see or feel anything.

"Tell me what to do," Ingrid says.

"The experiment is simple," Artemis explains. "You will step into the circle and let your magic flow into it. It will open the door. If my hypothesis is correct, Ruby will be there. If you see her, bring her back."

"How do I do that?" Ingrid asks.

"Don't concern yourself with the details," Artemis says.

Ingrid bites her lip, nervous, but gives a quick nod. She glances at me out of the corner of her eye, then quickly looks away.

"What do I do?" I ask.

"Observe and wait," Artemis says. She looks back to Ingrid. "Whenever you're ready."

Ingrid takes a deep breath, then looks at me and smiles.

"I hope this doesn't take too long," she says. "Dad says he's making tacos for dinner. All this magic stuff works up an appetite."

I stare at her, my heart lurching. She's not real, I know that. She's not my sister. She's an imposter in a body that looks like my sister. Once she's gone, I'll feel better knowing that I can try again to find the real Ingrid. It will be better not having someone living in my house with my sister's face and name. She never should have existed, so what does it matter if Ruby takes her body? It was never supposed to be hers to begin with.

But if that's true, why do I feel a terrible sense of dread?

"Here goes nothing," she says, and steps into the circle.

Immediately, the lines begin to glow, first green, then white. A harsh wind picks up around us, whipping my hair in front of my eyes, but the lines remain in place. Ingrid glows, her skin luminous in the whirlwind. She looks over her shoulder at me, and that look breaks my resolve.

"Wait—"

My voice is lost in the air that rushes all around us. I reach my hand through the turbulence to grab her, and it's like reaching into the tube of a vacuum cleaner. My skin feels whipped and raw, but I don't pull back. I reach for Ingrid, my fingers nearly gripping her clothes, when strong hands pull me back.

"Are you mad?" Artemis cries. "You can't enter the circle! You'll die!"

"We have to stop!" I shout, trying to pull my arms out of her grip. "We can't let her disappear!"

Artemis clenches tighter as I struggle.

"She's not real, Juniper!" Artemis says. "But Ruby is! Don't you see? This is my chance—Ruby's chance. I've been trying to get her back for fifty years. Fifty hopeless, agonizing years and now finally, *finally*, I have a chance at succeeding. I'm not letting you get in my way."

She drags me away from the circle. I try to rip my arms free, but it's no use. Ingrid's feet lift up. She hovers in the circle at the eye of the storm, three feet off the ground.

"Let her go, Juniper," Artemis says again. "You yourself said she wasn't real. You agreed!"

Artemis is right. I did agree. In my heart, though, I know that this is wrong. She grips me tighter, dragging me further from the circle.

There is a loud cracking sound, and the air around us chills. I look to my right just in time to see a large spike of ice shoot

247

from the ground. Artemis loses her grip on my arms, startled as she barely dodges the spike's sharp point.

Mateo stands just beyond the path, one foot sunken into the creek. His hands are covered with frost. Our eyes meet.

"Go!" he shouts.

Behind me, Artemis regains her balance, her attention drawn momentarily to Mateo.

"Do I know you?" she asks.

I don't wait to see if Mateo answers. I seize her distraction and lunge at the circle. The wind forms a barrier, but I push my way through with such force that I accidently topple into Ingrid and push her to the ground. Our bodies hit the dirt with a thud.

"Juniper, what are you—"

But I don't hear the rest of her question. My ears fill with the sound of Artemis screaming, and then everything fades to white.

Chapter 20

When I was in fourth grade, Ingrid got arrested.

Well, not exactly arrested. *Detained*. And cited for illegal collection of protected wildlife. She was only in sixth grade, and she was caught in the nature preserve with her butterfly gear. She'd done the impossible: she'd caught the Palos Verdes Blue.

But the park ranger saw her and made her release it. She started screaming at the ranger as she watched it flutter over the water and away, out of sight and out of reach. He threatened to call our parents, but she started throwing things at him, so he called the police instead.

I remember when they came home. I was doing my homework at the kitchen table when Dad brought her into the house. She tried to stomp upstairs, but he stopped her. I could hear them shouting from the den.

"There's no reason to catch one, Ingrid," he said. "Capturing an endangered species does nothing to advance science."

"It's not the same!" Ingrid shouted back. "It's not real!"

But what does it mean, to be real? Are the butterflies born in the butterfly house any less real than those raised in the wild? They're born, they eat, they metamorphosize, they die, just like the wild ones. Chemically and physiologically, they are the same.

They are real.

When I open my eyes, it looks like we are standing in a white room with white walls. But that's not right. There are no lines showing where the floor ends and the walls begin. There are no creases or corners. Everything is pure, empty white. Looking up and down, I feel dizzy. I can't tell left from right.

Ingrid stands beside me. Her hand is clenched in mine, but when she opens her eyes, she pulls away so fast, as if my hand was burning hers. She looks away and won't meet my eyes.

"Hello."

I look up. A girl stands before us. I didn't hear her walk up. It's like she appeared from nowhere. She doesn't look much older than me. She has short blond hair and a pointed nose. She wears an old-fashioned blouse, a pleated skirt, and a pair of polished black shoes. No one dresses like this unless they're going to a fifties party. She must be the girl Artemis is so determined to bring back.

"You're Ruby," I say.

Ingrid looks around, her voice shaking. "This is it, then? The magical plane?"

The girl named Ruby laughs. Her eyes sparkle.

"Not quite," she says. "You're not there yet. This is the in-between place."

"The in-between place?" I ask.

"It's hard to explain in a way you can understand." She shakes her head, then looks up at us. She cocks her head and narrows her eyes, as if she's trying to figure us out. "But you can't go further, can you?"

Ingrid and I look at each other.

"What do you mean?"

Ruby holds out her hands as if it's obvious.

"You're one, split into two."

Ingrid and I exchange nervous glances again.

"Do you mean we are the same person?" Ingrid asks.

Ruby doesn't answer. She lifts a gentle hand and places it on Ingrid's shoulder. Ingrid jumps, like an electric shock has gone through her. She stands up straighter, her hair on end. Ruby pulls her hand away, unfazed.

"You are pure magic." She turns to me and lifts her hand again. I brace for the shock, but none comes. Instead I feel a dull buzz, barely a hum. Ruby frowns.

"There's no magic in you at all," she says, lifting her hand. "You spit it all out. Want me to put it back?"

"What do you mean, put it back?" Ingrid cuts in.

Ruby shrugs. "Take whatever you are and put it back in her, of course," she says. "It's dangerous to let your magic run around wild like this, you know. I can put it back in, and you'll be back to normal. And then you can go to the magical plane. Why do you want to go to the magical plane anyway?"

"We're looking for you," Ingrid says.

Ruby laughs again. "Me? Why?"

"To bring you back, of course," Ingrid says.

Ruby looks thoughtful.

"Ah. Artemis is still trying to bring me back, is she? This is the furthest she's gotten, I reckon. How much time has passed? Two years? Three?"

"More like fifty-three," I say. "Maybe more."

Ruby's eyes widen.

"That long? Really? Time works differently here. I feel like I've been here a lifetime, but also that I just got here. I feel like I…"

She trails off, looking thoughtful again. Ingrid and I exchange pointed glances. I clear my throat.

"So the magical plane…it's real?"

"Oh yes," Ruby says. "Very real."

"What's it like?"

"It's marvelous," she says. "Everything I ever wondered about the world was answered. Every question about life and the universe. But they stopped mattering, because I realized there's so much more. Sure, I knew the answer of what happens after you die…but the things you see on the magical plane stop making you care about that kind of stuff. It's like learning there's a whole new world outside after being confined to your bedroom your entire life. It's not that any of those questions changed—I just started looking at them with a new perspective."

Anything I've ever wondered about life or the universe. Every answer to every scientific question known to humans. It all exists on the magical plane, and here I am, standing at its door. Ruby breaks out of her dreamy reverie and looks back at me.

"Shall I put you back together then, so you can come and see? Though once you are there, I do not think you will want to leave."

The answer to every question. The truth that every scientist ever wants. A new perspective, Ruby said.

I look at Ingrid. She is not really my sister, and never was. But when I look at her, I can't help seeing my real sister behind her eyes. More than anything I wish the real Ingrid were here, to tell me what I should choose. The real Ingrid was obsessed with science—she'd want the answers, maybe even do anything for them. Or would she? The real Ingrid was also kind and caring. She held my hand in the hard times. She was there for me.

This Ingrid—the fake Ingrid—is there for me too. Maybe she isn't like Ingrid. She doesn't care about science and wants to have friends other than me. But she also laughs at my jokes and wants to go to the beach.

Could I love her? Could I destroy her, if it meant learning the truth about the universe on the magical plane? If it meant collecting data that might lead me to the real Ingrid?

"I have to tell you something," I say.

Ingrid meets my eyes, confused. I swallow, the words lodged in my throat.

"You're not my sister. You're not real. I made you. Artemis says you're made of my memories and that your body is just like a human body, but that you're not really human. We were going to…we were going to try to put Ruby's soul in your body. But even though I know you're not my sister I just…I couldn't do it."

She stares at me for several moments. I sniff, my eyes stinging as I try to fight back tears. Then she puts a hand on my shoulder.

"I know," she says simply.

"You knew?"

"I suspected that I'm not really your sister. I was supposed to know about insects and like science and it just didn't feel… right. But I really liked some of the things we did. Riding bikes and watching movies and looking at the ocean. I don't know how to be a sister. I don't know how to be anything. But you loved me anyway. It's a new feeling for me…but I like it." She looks down. "I didn't say anything because I didn't want to lose you."

I laugh then. A real, hearty laugh. Ruby and Ingrid stare at me, but I can't stop laughing. Tears fill my eyes—tears of sadness, but tears of joy too.

"You really aren't my sister," I say.

Ingrid looks shocked. I wipe my eyes, but small bubbles of laughter escape from my lips.

"Ingrid would stand here and deliberate this question. She'd make a pros-and-cons list. She'd try to decide the difference between what's good for one person and what's good for humanity. If Ingrid were here, I think after a long while, she'd choose. And I'm honestly not sure if she'd choose her existence over science."

Fake Ingrid looks down at her hands, her long hair falling into face so I can't see her eyes. I reach out and I grab her hand.

"You're not Ingrid." I squeeze her fingers tight. "But that's not your fault. Some things can't be fixed… not even with magic."

Tears fall down the fake Ingrid's cheeks. I feel different, I realize. Lighter. I turn back to Ruby.

"I won't be going to the magical plane," I tell her. "And I'm sorry, but we can't bring you back either. We don't have a body for you."

"No, I can't go back to Earth. Not ever. And even if I could…" She looks up, in the direction of what would be the sky if we weren't in this plain white place. "I don't think I would want to."

"Can we go back?" I ask.

"I can send you back," she says. "After all, this is just the in-between place. I suppose it's a good thing you were split into two, otherwise you would've gone straight to the magical plane and never been able to return. Isn't that funny?"

She laughs for several uncomfortable moments. I try not to look as horrified as I feel.

"Will you give Artemis a message, though? I hate that she's torn herself apart over this for so many decades."

"Of course."

Ruby puts one hand on my shoulder and one hand on Ingrid's. She stares into my eyes, and the world begins to blur again.

"Tell her I said I'm already home."

When I open my eyes, Ingrid and I are back in the nature preserve standing in the dirt circle. Artemis hovers above the creek, water rushing below her. Her clothes are soaked and sagging. There is a figure on the ground beside the creek, struggling to stand up.

Mateo.

Artemis lifts her hands. She looks otherworldly, hovering over the creek. Bubbles of water hover around her. Mateo rolls over onto his hands and knees and coughs. Shards of ice litter the ground around him.

She stops when she sees us. It's like time freezes: the drops of water that surrounded her halt in midair. Her eyes fall on Ingrid, and she starts to move toward us, levitating like a ghost. She stops right in front of Ingrid and drops to the ground, her mouth quivering into a hesitant smile.

"Ruby?" she asks quietly. "Is that you?"

"Ruby told me to tell you that she's already home," Ingrid says. "She's not coming back."

Artemis's smile falters.

"Impossible," she says, her voice a low, dangerous whisper. "Of course she wants to come back."

"She doesn't," I say. "She said she's found her home. It's up there, wherever that is. She told us to tell you to stop trying to bring her back."

"How do you know?" Artemis shouts. Ingrid and I flinch back. "You don't know her! You don't know what she's been through!"

Artemis's hands shake. Her whole body shakes with anger. Tears fall down her cheeks. This is the first time I've seen Artemis cry. But when she looks back up, she doesn't look sad. She looks livid.

"She didn't even know how much time had passed," I say. "She doesn't want to come back. It's too good up there, she says. She has all the secrets of the universe. She doesn't want to be on Earth anymore."

"I do not accept this!" Artemis cries. "I'm going to get Ruby back! I promised I would!"

She lifts her hands, dark plumes of smoke rising from her palms. My eyes burn, like I'm sitting too close to a campfire. I lift my arm to cover my face and feel something brush past my feet. I catch a glimpse of a bushy, striped tail.

It's a strange sight to see Soren the lemur standing in front of Artemis. He's only as tall as my thigh when he stands on his back legs, and his body looks so slim and fragile in front of her. Artemis, on the other hand, looks terrifying. She's floating again. Her arms are spread, and dark clouds of smoke and lightning fill the air behind her. But Soren is unafraid.

"Stop this." His voice is cool and calm in the face of Artemis's fury, but she is unfazed. "Josephine, I said stop."

My breath catches at the mention of Artemis's real name. I wonder how long it's been since she's gone by that name—how long the two of them have really been practicing magic in the Elm House. It makes me realize there's so much I don't know about them.

Artemis looks down on him.

"What did you call me?"

Soren doesn't answer. There is a bright glow as his body begins to shift and change. The formless shape grows larger and larger, until he's no longer Soren the lemur—he's Soren the man.

Soren is the same height as Artemis, or maybe a tad shorter. Long hair cascades past his shoulders. He wears an old-fashioned, charcoal gray suit. His face is recognizable from the portrait on the stairs in the Elm House. This is Soren's true form.

"Look around at what you are doing," he says. "Look at all the people you're hurting, and for what?"

"For Ruby!" Artemis screams.

Soren cocks his head, exactly the way he used to do when he was a lemur. He holds out a hand to Artemis.

258

"Come down, my love," he says calmly. "I didn't attain immortality with you so that you could live in the past. We did it to live in the future."

The wind whips harder than before. Lightning flashes in Artemis's cloud of anger. But Soren is unmoved. He keeps his hand held out to her.

"It's time to let go."

Lightning cracks, splitting the sky in two. I think for sure that Artemis will strike Soren down. But then the black smoke dissipates, and Artemis floats down to the ground. Soren bends down and places a hand on her back. She buries her face in his shoulder, and he wraps his arms around her.

I let go of Ingrid and go to Mateo, who is still on the ground. He pushes himself up to his feet, coughing. His clothes are soaked to his skin. The pendant dangles around his neck.

"Are you all right?" I ask.

"I'm fine," he says, but his voice sounds strained. He follows my gaze and tucks the pendant back in his shirt. "I never know when I'll need it."

"You saved me again," I say. "Sorry."

"Now you owe me," he says, then winces, clutching at his ribs. "My tía is going to kill me."

"Maybe Soren can help," I say.

But when I turn around, Soren, Artemis, and Ingrid are gone.

When I walk into my house around sunset, covered in dirt and scrapes, Mom drops a pan of taquitos with a clatter on the stove and runs to me. She grabs my shoulders with her oven mitts and looks me over.

"Juniper, what on Earth happened to you?" she asks.

I open my mouth to come up with some sort of excuse, but I can't. Instead, tears well up in my eyes, and I let them fall. My mom looks at me like I'm a freak alien creature, but only for a second. She pulls me into a tight hug.

"Hey, it's okay, June, you're not in trouble," she says gently. "Shh, it's okay, I'm here. What's wrong?"

"I miss Ingrid," I cry, muffled by her shoulder.

Mom pats the back of my head with one of her oven mitts. For a moment, I'm afraid she'll wonder what's wrong with me. Doesn't she think Ingrid is alive?

Instead she pulls me tighter.

"I know, sweetheart, I know," she says, her voice cracking. "I miss Ingrid too."

Hearing her say the words makes me cry even harder. But in some twisted way, it also makes me feel better. Mom pulls away just enough to kiss me on the forehead.

"Shh, it's okay," she whispers between my eyes. "Why don't we talk about it?"

PART VII
Conclude

Chapter 21

When I walk into science class the next day, I don't go to my normal seat at my lab table. Instead I walk right up to Mrs. Cartwright.

"I'm sorry," I say.

She cocks an eyebrow at me.

"The apology isn't supposed to be for me," she says.

"I think you deserve one too," I tell her. "I know I haven't been the easiest student to deal with."

She smiles at me kindly.

"Maybe not," she admits. "But you're passionate about science, which can be rare. That nearly makes up for it."

"I have a favor to ask." I hold up the rolled-up poster. "I would like to redo my presentation. It's part of my apology, for Chelsea."

Mrs. Cartwright purses her lips and checks the clock.

"I suppose we have a few extra minutes, since we're not doing any lab work today. But make it quick."

I nod and go straight to the front of the classroom. The bell rings just as the last few students take their seats. From the back of the room, I see Chelsea sitting with her arms crossed. Her eyes are narrowed suspiciously. Normally I would avoid her gaze, but this time I nod at her.

"Juniper has a short presentation, and then we will get started," Mrs. Cartwright says from her desk. "I don't want to hear any talking. Go ahead, Juniper."

I clear my throat, just like my dad does, more as a way to indicate I'm about to start than to actually clear anything from my throat. I grip the poster tightly in my hands. I didn't actually plan out what I am going to say, so I think about what Dad said to me at the dinner table last night. I imagine I'm him, and that this is a class of passionate college students I'm about to lecture to.

"Science is a way to learn more about the world. When we study science, we answer questions and get a greater understanding. But that understanding is meaningless without our appreciation of the world around us."

I unroll the poster and quickly clip it to the board.

The poster looks nothing like our original presentation, which was mostly typed pages and a few photos squished at the bottom. I removed the pages, revealing Chelsea's sketches of the wildlife she saw at the nature preserve. I put back the photos that

I'd ripped off. I even added a few sketches of my own, some that survived in notebooks I didn't bring with me on that day I fell into the creek.

"Sometimes when we talk about science it's easy to get bogged down by all the scientific terms. We forget why we study it in the first place. To understand. We're all a part of the world, and there are a lot of reasons to study it. There are a million reasons, but one of them is that nature is beautiful. It's...poetic even."

I look at Mateo when I say it, and he grins at me. I glance over to Chelsea, and I see her eyes have lit up as she leans forward in her seat, straining to see the poster. I want to be done, but there's something missing. Something I still have to do.

"When we did our presentations before, I forgot how beautiful the world is, and I focused too much on facts. So this poster highlights some really cool aspects about nature. My partner, Chelsea, drew most of these sketches. She's really good at that. I'm sorry you didn't get to see them before."

Chelsea looks at me, then, and her eyes look watery. She turns red and looks away. She's not glaring at me, though, so I suppose that's a good sign.

The other kids in the class are all looking at the drawings on the poster. I look at Mrs. Cartwright, and she looks pleased.

"Thank you, Juniper," Mrs. Cartwright says. "That was very well done."

"There's one more thing." I reach into my pocket and pull out a folded piece of notebook paper. "I wrote something about the nature preserve. It's my favorite place."

I clear my throat and read:

> Dusty hills and coastal oak,
> Wings of blue and brown and gold,
> Salt air and bright sun,
> The wonder of nature to behold.
> Some capture beauty in paintings
> And others in a net.
> It's all a type of magic
> For everyone to get.

There is a moment of quiet, and then someone claps, followed by the rest of the class. I feel my face turn bright red.

"Um, that's all," I mumble. I leave the poster clipped up and go sit in my seat. Mateo flashes me a thumbs-up, and I smile at him.

It was hard to stand up there and admit that I was wrong. But sometimes scientists get things wrong—they use the wrong calculations, or the data gets corrupted. I definitely miscalculated with Chelsea and Mateo, and Ingrid too.

Not everything can be fixed—but some things can.

I spend the next few weeks in a calm sort of quiet. Just as no one remembered that Ingrid had died when I brought her back, now no one remembers that she was momentarily alive again. It's as if all the same events of the past few weeks happened, but Ingrid is absent, carefully removed from everyone's memory. I don't know if it's another glamour or just the old one wearing off.

It feels strange walking by the Elm House every day and seeing all the windows dark. I still stop at the gate and look, hoping to catch a glimpse of a shadow in the highest window or a striped tail disappearing over a garden wall. But the house lies abandoned.

With no mysterious house to sneak off to, I find it hard to fill my time. Most days I go over to Mateo's house or he comes over to mine, and we talk alternately about poetry and bugs. Sometimes both. And sometimes Mateo starts to teach me magic, the beginner's way. I can't grow flowers out of pencils anymore, but maybe one day I'll be able to turn a stick into a rose.

One day, as Mateo and I are walking home from school, something is different about the Elm House. The padlock normally holding the front gate closed is gone, and the gate sits slightly open. Mateo and I stand in front of it.

"What do you think it means?" I ask.

"Maybe the city is finally going to demolish it," Mateo says.

"I hope not." The voice comes from behind the large elm tree. Ingrid steps into view. I almost didn't recognize her—her hair is cut short and she's wearing a zip-up hoodie and jeans. I stare at her. It's been several weeks since Artemis tried to use her body to bring Ruby back, and I haven't seen her since.

"Hey," she says finally, giving me a shy wave.

"I'll get going," Mateo says. "Come over later, okay?"

Mateo slips out the gate. I walk over to where Ingrid stands beneath the elm tree.

"Your hair looks nice," I say, the only thing I can think of.

"Thanks," she says, reaching up to touch the ends. "I wanted something different. More me. Besides, I don't want to freak your parents out."

"Are you staying around?"

"I want to," she says. "I like life here. School and friends and food, it's all amazing. Though I suppose everything's amazing when I've never experienced it before."

"I bet," I say. "Where are Artemis and Soren?"

"England. That's where we've been the past few weeks," she explains. "They have a house there—apparently they've owned it for over a hundred years, can you believe it?"

"I'd believe anything," I say truthfully.

"I didn't like it," she says. "It rained the whole time. I missed the sunshine. I missed—"

She stops short.

"Do you hate me?" she asks quietly.

"No," I say. "But…I don't know you. I think I'd like to."

"I don't know me, either. I'm going to start over. Artemis and Soren are going to come back, eventually, but they aren't going to hide. We're going to pretend to be moving into the neighborhood.

I'll start over—I'll be a new me. I've already got the hair, and now I just need a new name."

"Like what?"

"I have a few ideas," she says. "Do you know how hard it is to pick your own name? I'm totally overthinking it."

We laugh. I thought I would be sad seeing her here, but the more time passes, the less I see her as Ingrid.

"I might not be your sister," she continues, "but I'd be happy to be your friend."

I used to think I didn't need friends, but it turns out having them is not so bad.

"I would like that."

"One more thing." She reaches into her pocket and pulls out a small metal box. "This is yours."

She flips open the lid and holds it out to me. I gasp. Inside, I see familiar gossamer wings. A Palos Verdes Blue. A small hole punctuates the middle of the butterfly's abdomen, and I know it's the same one I took from my dad's display case. I reach out and take the box carefully into my hands.

"But how?" I ask.

"A little magic of my own."

I close the lid.

"Thank you."

She opens her mouth, then hesitates.

"What?" I ask.

"I never knew your sister," she says slowly. "But I am filled

271

with your memories of her. And even though you didn't catch the Blue, I think that she would have been proud of you."

A strange pressure builds up behind my eyes. She's right—I didn't catch the Blue. I didn't accomplish the one thing Ingrid wanted more than anything. But after all this time, I did something Ingrid couldn't do—something Dad told her to do over and over again, something that she could never fully grasp.

I let it go.

Epilogue

TWO MONTHS LATER

In the early hours of the morning, I creep down the stairs in socked feet, careful to skip the squeaky steps so I don't wake my parents. I make my way into the den. Dull gray light greets me through the sheer curtain of the window.

I cross the room to Dad's desk and pull the chain of the lamp. It clatters on, illuminating the cases of insects lining the walls. There's one case, smaller than the rest, that's mine. I press my fingers gently to the glass and read the carefully scrawled words my sister wrote years ago:

G. lygdamus palosverdesensis

But the space above it is no longer empty. A small butterfly the color of cornflower and no bigger than my thumbnail is pinned carefully in the space. It's not real—it's made of carefully woven silk. Dad bought it for me on Etsy. I never caught a wild one. I figure I'll let the wild ones be wild. And the ones that happen to be born inside a butterfly house instead of under the blue sky, well—they're just as good, and just as worthy of love.

I spend the morning poring over my notebooks and trail maps. After losing all my notes, I've been putting together something even better. The work lives in a large, leather-bound notebook Mom got me from the museum gift shop. It's unlike anything I've ever used before. The leather cover is soft and has jagged edges, and there's a cord that wraps around it instead of a clasp. The pages are cream-colored and don't have lines. But the best part is that I'm not the only one writing in it anymore.

Mom and Dad eventually get up, moving slowly since it's Saturday morning. By the time they amble into the kitchen to make coffee, I'm already downing a bowl of cereal. I'm wearing my khaki shorts and my boots, and even my oversized SAVE THE PALOS VERDES BLUE T-shirt. My binoculars bounce against my chest as I put my bowl in the sink.

"Going out again today?" Dad asks, reaching out to ruffle my hair. I dodge his hand and pick the notebook off the table.

"Yep! I told Isabelle I'd meet her at her house."

"Oh, you should ask her parents how the remodel is going," Mom says.

"Will do!" I grab my backpack and head out the door. "See you later!"

I walk down my driveway and around the hedges until I'm standing in front of the Elm House. The tall, wrought-iron gate has been replaced with a white, suburban-looking fence. I undo the latch and walk up the path. The heavy metal knocker is still there, but I use the modern electronic doorbell.

The girl that answers is not Ingrid, and she's stopped pretending to be. She goes by Isabelle now. Even with different hair, she still looks a lot like my sister. But as she gets older, she looks less and less like her every day. Without the expectation of living up to my sister's memory, we can just be friends.

Isabelle grins when she sees me.

"I just need to get my camera," she says, and she runs up the stairs.

Soren and Artemis appear through the kitchen door.

"Morning, Juniper," Soren says. Artemis stands by his side, their arms linked at the elbows. Artemis and Soren look like regular neighbors on a Saturday morning—because they are. They aren't dressed in their usual vintage Victorian garb. Artemis wears a blue velvet track suit, and Soren has on jeans and a short-sleeve button-down shirt with frogs printed on it.

They decided to lift the glamour on the Elm House. Well, most of it. Since everyone thought it'd been abandoned for years, they're pretending to be a small family that's moving in and renovating the place. While there are still many things that need to be cloaked in order to keep magic a secret, they were sick of hiding. Isabelle found a home by pretending to be their daughter. When they came over to formally introduce themselves, my parents definitely saw the resemblance. They have no memories of those few weeks where I'd thought I'd brought her back to life. It's better that way.

"Juniper, I was wondering—tomorrow, would you like to come study the magical properties of lavender root?" Artemis asks. "I can make scones."

"That sounds fun," I say. I don't have the magic I used to have, but that doesn't mean magic is blocked off to me. I just have to learn it the hard way—through long, arduous study.

Isabelle returns from upstairs. Her camera hangs around her neck.

"Ready!"

I wave goodbye to Artemis and Soren. Isabelle and I ride our bikes down the street to Mateo's house. He's already outside, his helmet pressing down his blob of hair. He's got his nose buried in a Robert Frost book.

"Hey," he says, tucking his book away. "Did you bring the notebook?"

"Of course," I say.

We wave to Tía Barbara, who stands in the doorway, and ride our bikes to the nature preserve. At the gate where sidewalk turns to trail, Chelsea waits for us on her bike too. She's wearing purple striped tights that match the new purple streak in her hair.

"Did you bring the journal?" she asks as we roll up.

"Of course!" I roll my eyes.

We hop off our bikes and walk them down the trail. Isabelle starts snapping pictures with her camera.

"The lighting is perfect," she mutters.

It's an overcast June morning, cool but comfortable, the heat of summer not yet setting in. I pull the leather journal out of my backpack and flip it open.

The pages are filled not just with my normal scientific notes, but with page after page of art, poetry, and photos. Isabelle, Mateo, Chelsea, and I have been passing this notebook back and forth, each of us adding our own observations to it in our own way. Chelsea holds out her hands.

"It's my week," she says.

Mateo sidles up next to her.

"I thought you had it last week," he says. "It's my turn."

"I didn't! Isabelle had it. You're after me."

I hand it to her, and she flips to the next blank page. Before I say anything else, she has her colored pencils out. She crouches down and starts to sketch a small brown bunny, frozen just a few feet away.

Mateo shrugs and pulls a small notepad out of his pocket. I have my own notepad. I can always add my own notes to the journal later.

That's been our big project the past few months. Isabelle takes photos, Mateo writes poems, Chelsea draws, and I do what I do best—observe and record. The contents might not be the most scientific, but they reflect how we feel about this nature preserve, and that has a lot more truth to it.

Mateo wanders off to find a nice place to sit and write. I close my eyes and take a deep breath. The morning air is fresh and fragrant, and I can smell the salt of the ocean just beyond the cliffs. I listen to the songbirds chirp in the brush and the sound of distant waves crashing against the shore. I hear the click of Isabelle's camera and the scratch of Chelsea's pencils. I've always loved the nature preserve—but it's even better with friends.

I open my eyes. Right in front of me, a light blue butterfly lands on a milkweed. I recognize it immediately. A Palos Verdes Blue. Its gossamer wings open and shut, and then, a moment later, it lifts off and flutters through the air. I grin and watch it fly away.

Acknowledgments

This book would not exist without the village of friends, family, colleagues, and collaborators who helped bring it to life.

Thank you to my editor, Nivair Gabriel, who understood my vision of balancing science and magic from the beginning, and to the rest of the Albert Whitman team for believing in this story. I would also like to thank my agent, Travis Pennington, and everyone at the Knight Agency.

I am very appreciative of Dr. Michael Toliver for his expert advice on entomology.

I would like to thank my family for always supporting my writing, especially my mom, Victoria, and my brother, Aidan. Thank you to Roger and Penelope, who watched this book grow from a tiny seed into what it is today.

I am especially thankful for Paige Gulley, who helped me through my toughest moments and is an unending source of inspiration and encouragement.

Thank you to the writers in my life who made this lonely hobby into a community. I'm so lucky to know so many talented and supportive writers. This book would not be possible without the Barmies, especially Eddie Louise, Chip Clark, AnnMarie Gomez, An Dang, Mike Philips, Justin Bremer, Lara Ameen, Shannon Villegas, Gwen Kress, and Lynn Yu, who slogged alongside me in coffee shops and donut joints and Swedish furniture stores. I would also like to thank my Idyllwild Arts family, who will always have a place in my heart, especially Kim Henderson, Andrew Leeson, Becky Hirsch, and Austin Okopny. I would also like to thank Mia Siegert, Elliot Grinnell, and José Ángel for their generous advice and support.

I am eternally grateful to my Friday-night D&D crew, who taught me more about story—and myself—than I ever could have imagined: Alison Clifford, Sara Lagan, Khadra Zerouali, Justine Garcia, Quincy Balius, and Eliza Vasquez.

Thank you to the friends who have supported me in more ways than I can count, especially Destiny and Rod Conwi, Lawrence and Rachel Cox, Alyssa Beach, Martin Knobel, Jordan Myers, Kha Nguyen, Alison Zalk, Ken Fernandez, and Ryan Birchfield, just to name a few.

Finally, I want to thank all the selfless library workers I have had the honor of working alongside. You make the world a better place.